Barrington Stoke
School Spelling Dictionary

Christine Maxwell and Julia Rowlandson

Barrington Stoke

First published in Great Britain by Barrington Stoke Ltd,
18 Walker Street, Edinburgh, EH3 7LP

www.barringtonstoke.co.uk

Dictionary of Perfect Spelling copyright © 2005 Christine Maxwell

Barrington Stoke School Spelling Dictionary produced under license

Copyright © 2007 Barrington Stoke

This edition published in 2012
Reprinted 2013

The moral right of the author has been asserted in accordance with
the Copyright, Designs and Patents Acts 1988

ISBN: 978-1-78112-151-1

Cover design by Rich Carr

Trademarks
Words in this dictionary which we believe to be trademarks have
been acknowledged as such. The presence or absence of such
acknowledgements should not be regarded as affecting the legal
status of any trademarks or proprietary name.

Typeset by GreenGate Publishing Services, Tonbridge TN9 2RN
Printed in Great Britain by Charlesworth Press

Acknowledgements

I would like to thank the following people:

Christine Maxwell for having the original insight into creating a dictionary that can be easily used by poor spellers.

All the children who contributed misspellings which often in their opinion were how the words should be spelt!

My late father, David Driver, who tirelessly checked head words with me.

Ruth Paris for her patient editorial work and sense of humour.

Kate MacPhee and Joanna Craddock for their proof-reading skills.

Julia Rowlandson BA Hons, PGCE, Dip RSA, SpLD

Preface

To the Teacher

After the publication of the revised and updated *Dictionary of Perfect Spelling*, Barrington Stoke has had numerous requests for a school version.

In my work as Head of English in a school for boys with specific learning difficulties, I continually witnessed the frustrations of children trying to use a conventional dictionary to help with their spelling. More often or not they gave up and spelt the word phonically. In the *School Spelling Dictionary*, following Christine Maxwell's inspirational idea, they can do just this.

But when they check their phonic spelling, if they find the word in red, it is wrong and beside it they will find the correct spelling in black.

For example: eny   any

They can then locate the correct spelling and check any derivatives.

For example: any ~body ~how ~one

         any ~thing ~way ~where

The tilde(~) tells the user to just add on the ending to the root word.

Irregular plurals are given.

For example: wolf wolves

Verb endings are given in full.

For example: fly [flies flying flew flown]

Comparative adjectives are spelt out.

For example: funny funnier funniest

If they have difficulty finding a word, there are hints as to where else to look.

For example: Under **ci** you will find

Check out si as well

I have included some useful spelling rules which need to be taught and learnt. I found Gill Cotterell's Phonic Reference cards published by LDA an excellent resource.

To the Speller!

The English language is very hard for the person who hates spelling because groups of letters can make more than one sound. Even spell checkers find it hard! However, 86% of words do stick to rules and the tips on pages v to vii are there to help you. We call the other 14% of words 'irregular' because they do not follow rules or patterns and you need to find ways to remember them.
Pages viii to x will give you some ideas of ways to learn them.

We all need to spell words the same way to make sure that we can write what we want to say and so everyone who reads it can understand exactly what we mean.

Some Useful English Spelling Rules –
It does help to learn them!!

1. Remember vowels (a e i o u) can make a short sound or a long sound (like their name).
   For example ā as in ape [long – its name], ă as in apple [short – its sound].
   ' y' sometimes acts as a vowel as well, e.g. ' cry' and ' rhythm' .

2. Have fun with words! Learn to build words from the root word, use **prefixes** (bits you add on the front) and **suffixes** (bits you add on the end).
   For example: stand, <u>under</u>stand, understand<u>ing</u>, <u>misunder</u>standing

3. 'q' always has 'u' with it and is written 'qu' like in 'quiz' and 'question'.

4. No word ends in ' v' except ' spiv' (a flashy man). Often ' e' comes after ' v' to prop it up like in ' active' and ' native'.

5. No word ends in 'j'.

6. Never write a 'k' before a 't'. Always write 'ct' as in 'fact' and 'direct'.

7. No English word ends in 'i'.
   Watch out for rule breakers: taxi (short for taxicab) and ski, spaghetti and macaroni (but they aren't English!).

8. The 'ee' sound at the end of a word is mostly spelt 'y'.
   Watch out for rule breakers: coffee and committee!

9. Double 'l' 'f' and 's' after a single vowel in a short word, e.g. spell, boss, stiff, puff. Watch out for rule breakers: us, bus, gas, if, of, this, yes, plus, nil, pal!

10. Add 's' to make a regular plural as in 'cat - cats'.

11. Add 'es' to make a plural if the word has a hissing ending like: 's - buses, x - foxes, sh - brushes, ch - churches, ss – fusses.

12. If a word ends in one 'f', change it to 'v' and add 'es' to make the plural.
    For example: leaf ➤ leav ➤ leaves, wolf ➤ wolv ➤ wolves.
    Watch out for rule breakers: dwarfs, chiefs, roofs!

13. For most words that end in 'o', add 'es' to make the plural. For example: potato + es = potatoes.
    Watch out for rule breakers: pianos, solos, Eskimos!

14. The prefix 'all' at the start of a word is only spelt with one 'l' – almost, altogther, also, already.

15. The suffixes 'full and till' at the end of the word only have one 'l' – helpful, until.

16. Remember the suffix to make an adverb is 'ly' NOT 'ley'!

17. Drop the final 'e' from the root word before adding a suffix that starts with a vowel. For example: move + ed = moved, like + ing = liking, drive + er = driver, muddle + ed = muddled.

18. If a word ends in a consonant + y, change the 'y' to 'i' before adding any ending except 'ing'. For example:
marry + es = marries, funny + ly = funnily.
BUT fly – ing = flying, carry - ing = carrying.

19. 'ck', 'dge', 'tch' are used after a short vowel (one that says its sound). For example: back, hedge, match.
Watch out for rule breakers: rich, much, such, which!

20. If a words ends in a single vowel and a single consonant always double the final consonant before adding a suffix that starts with a vowel.
For example: stop + ed = stopped, fat + er = fatter, hot + est = hottest, rob + ing = robbing.

21. 'ce', 'ci', 'cy' makes the /s/ sound.
For example: centre, circle, cycle.

22. 'ge', 'gi', 'gy' makes the /j/ sound.
For example: gentle, giant, gym.
Watch out for rule breakers: get, begin, girl, give, gear, geese, gift, girth!

23. 'i' comes before 'e' except after c, but not when it sounds like /ā/ as in 'neighbour' and 'weigh'.
Watch out for rule breakers: neither, foreign, seized, sovereign, forfeit!

Ways to Learn Spellings

Hear it 👂 See it 👁 Say it 👄 Do it ✋

To remember a spelling you must –

1. Think about the word that you are trying to learn and make sure you understand what it means.
2. Divide it into syllables (chunks). You can find where they are by putting your hand under your chin and counting how many times your chin goes down when you say the word.
   For example: Sat/ur/day = 3 syllables. Note that each syllable must have a vowel. It can sometimes be 'y'.
3. Talk about which parts of the word are hard to spell and highlight them.
4. Practise spelling the word at odd times, e.g. on the way to school, in the shower/bath, etc.
5. Learn other words with the same pattern and then they will be easier to remember. For example:
   few, crew, grew, flew, blew, etc.
6. Use the learning style you like best.

👂 If you are an auditory person: – say it aloud to yourself, sing it, turn it into a rap, quiz a friend.

👁 If you are a visual person practise write it; use different colours, look at the tall letters and short letters, draw pictures as clues, pretend your eyes are a camera and take a photo of it. Can you see a little word inside it?

✋ If you are a person who likes to learn by doing things, make huge letters in the air, walk up and down chanting it, do an action which links to the word, decide how many sounds are in the word and with the palm of your hand facing you, touch a finger as you say each sound.

7. For irregular words, think of associations/mnemonics to trigger your memory. Remember, the more ridiculous your rhyme, the easier it is to remember how to spell the word.

8. Talk about it and teach it to a friend or to a parent.

Let's learn to spell the word *'people'* using a technique with a very long name – 'Neuro-linguistic Programming' or NLP for short.

1. Ask your teacher to write *people* on a card in large lower case letters

2. Talk about the bit which make it hard to learn – You can't hear the o and you have to remember the /pul/ sound at the end is spelt *'ple'*

3. Now look up to the left and visualise (imagine you can see) the first letter *p* in the air or on a wall (you can choose a colour for it)

4. Now say *p* aloud

5. Now visualise the next letter *e* beside it

6. Start at the beginning and say the two letters aloud *pe*

7. Now say them backwards *ep*

   We do this to make sure you are visualising *pe*. You will find it hard to say it backwards if you are not visualising the letters

8. Then add the next letter, that silent one *o*. Pretend you are climbing through the circle it makes

9. Now say them from the beginning *peo* and backwards *oep*

10. Now add another *p*. Make sure it is the same size and colour as the first one

11. What do you have in the air now? Say *peop* and then backwards *poep*

12. Now add a tall *l*

13. What do you have? *peopl*   *lpoep*

14. Now for the last letter. Add another *e* in the same colour as the first *e*

15. What do you have? *people*. Backwards *elpoep*

16. Brilliant! Write it down

17. Now write a short sentence using it

18. Test yourself later in the day. If you think you have forgotten how to spell the word, look up to the left to help recall it. Then write another short sentence using the word.

19. Practise it every day for a week and keep your own spelling bank!

It really works!

abacus

abandon

  [abandoning abandoned]

abawt   about

abbey

abcent   absent

abdamen   abdomen

abdomen

abee   abbey

abel   able

ability   abilities

able

abnormal   abnormally

abolish [abolishing abolished]

Aboriginal   Aborigine

about

above

abowt   about

abracadabra

abrawd   abroad

abroad

absail   abseil

absant   absent

absawb   absorb

abseil [abseiling abseiled]

absence

absent   absent-minded

abserd   absurd

absorb [absorbing absorbed]

absorbent

absurd   absurdly

abuse [abusing abused]

abuv   above

abyus   abuse

accelerate

   [accelerating accelerated]

accelerator   acceleration

accent

accept *[take]   except *[but]

   [accepting accepted]

acceptance

accident

accidental   accidentally

accommodation

account [accounting accounted]

accountant

accross   across

accur   occur

accurate   accurately

accuse [accusing accused]

ace

acelerate   accelerate

acent   accent

acept   accept

ache [aching ached]   achy

acheive   achieve

1

achieve achievement
[achieving achieved]
acid acid rain

Check out acc as well

acident   accident
acksel   axel *[jump]
               axil *[leaf]
               axle *[wheel]
acne
acorn
acownt   account
acre acreage
acrobat acrobatic
across
acselerate   accelerate
acsent   accent
acsept   accept
acshun   action
acsident   accident
act [acting acted]
actchely   actually
acter   actor
action action-packed
active actively
activetys   activities
activity activities

actor actress actresses
actual actually
acurate   accurate
acuse   accuse
acute acutely
ad *[advert]   add *[sum]
Adam's apple
adapt [adapting adapted]
adaptable
add *[sum]   ad *[advert]
[adding added]
addapt   adapt
addenoyds   adenoids
adder
addict [addicted] addiction
addition *[sum]   edition *[copy]
additional
additive
addoor   adore
address addresses
[addressing addressed]
ade   aid
adenoids
ader   adder
adhesive
adishun   addition
adjective
adjust adjustable

2

admier   admire

admiral

admire [admiring admired]

admiration

admit [admitting admitted]

admyre   admire

adopt   adoption

adorable

adore [adoring adored]

adress   address

adult

advance

  [advancing advanced]

advantage

advencher   adventure

adventure   adventurous

adverb

advertise

  [advertising advertised]

advertisement

advice *[a tip]   advise *[suggest]

advise *[suggest]   advice *[a tip]

  [advising advised]

advurb   adverb

advurtise   advertise

ael   ale

aer   air

aerial

Check out air as well

aerodrome

aeroplane

aerosol

aery   airy

afar *[long]   affair *[event]

afect   affect *[alter]

       effect *[result]

affair

affect *[alter]   effect *[result]

affection   affectionate

affectionately

affekshun   affection

afford   affordable

affraede   afraid

afid   aphid

afloat

aford   afford

afraid

after

afternoon

afterwards

aftr   after

again

against

agane   again

age [ageing aged]

agectiv — adjective

agene — again

aggression

aggressive aggressively

agile

ago

agony agonies

agre — agree

agree [agreeing agreed]

agreeable

agreement

agreshun — aggression

agresiv — aggressive

agriculcher — agriculture

agriculture

aground

ahead

aid [aiding aided]

aim aimless aimlessly

air *[gas] — heir *[inherits]

air-conditioning

aircraft aircraft carrier

airea — area

air ~fare ~field ~lift

air ~line ~mail ~raid

airial — aerial

airodrome — aerodrome

airoplane — aeroplane

airosol — aerosol

airport

airy

ais — ace

aisle *[passage] — isle *[island]

ajar

ajective — adjective

ajile — agile

ajust — adjust

ake — ache

Check out ac as well

akselerayt — accelerate

akshun — action

aksident — accident

akt — act

aktiv — active

aktor — actor

Alah — Allah

alarm

alastik — elastic

album

alcohol alcoholic

ale

alein — alien

alert [alerting alerted]

alevan eleven

alfabet alphabet

algae

algebra

algee algae

alian alien

alien

aligator alligator

alight

alike

alite alight

aliterashun alliteration

alive

aljebra algebra

alkaline

alkohol alcohol

all all right

Allah

allarm alarm

allergic allergic reaction

allergy allergies

allert alert

alley *[path] ally *[friend]

alligator

alliteration

allmost almost

allot *[give] a lot *[many]

allotment

allow [allowing allowed]

allowed *[may] aloud *[talk]

alltho although

alltogether altogether

allurgic allergic

allwase always

allways always

ally *[friend] alley *[path]

almond

almost

aloan alone

alone

along alongside

a lot *[many] allot *[give]

aloud *[talk] allowed *[may]

alowed allowed *[may]
aloud *[talk]

alphabet alphabetical

Alps alpine

already

Alsation

also

altar *[church]

alter *[change] [altering altered]

alteration

alternative alternatively

although

althow although

altitude

altogether

alurt   alert

always

aly   ally *[friend]

         alley *[path]

alyke   alike

alyve   alive

am

amaze   amazement

Amazon

ambassador

ambel   amble

ambishun   ambition

ambition

ambitious

amble [ambling ambled]

amboosh   ambush

ambulance

ambush   ambushes

ame   aim

ameeba   amoeba

amen

amethyst

amfibian   amphibian

amfibious   amphibious

ammaze   amaze

ammunition

ammuse   amuse

amoeba

among   amongst

amount

amp

amphibian   amphibious

amputate   amputation

    [amputating amputated]

amung   among

amunishun   ammunition

amuse   amusement

amythist   amethyst

an

anagram

anceint   ancient

ancestor

anchor

ancient

ancor   anchor

and

anemone

aneversary   anniversary

anex   annexe

aney   any

angel *[God]   angle *[maths]

angelic   angelically

anger

angle *[maths]   angel *[God]

angler
Anglo-Saxon
angree   angry
angrily
angry angrier angriest
angur   anger
angziety   anxiety
animal
animation
animel   animal
aniseed
aniversary   anniversary
anjel   angel
ankel   ankle
ankle
ankor   anchor
ankshus   anxious
anmils   animals
annalise   analyse
annexe
anniversary anniversaries
annonymous   anonymous
annorak   anorak
annother   another
announce announcement
annoy [annoying annoyed]
annual annually
anonymous anonymously

anorak
another
anownce   announce
anoy   annoy
ansed   answered
anser   answer
ansestor   ancestor
anshent   ancient
answer [answering answered]
ant *[insect]   aunt *[family]
Antarctic Antarctica
antebyotic   antibiotic

Check out anti as well

anteclimacks anticlimax
anteek   antique
antehistameen antihistamine
antelope
antenna antennae
antesoshall   antisocial
anthology anthologies
antibiotic
antic *[prank]   antique *[old]
anticeptic   antiseptic
anticlimax
anticlockwise
antihistamine

antilope   antelope

antique *[old]   antic *[prank]

antiseptic

antisocial   antisocially

antler

antonym

anual   annual

anuther   another

anuver   another

anxiety   anxieties

anxious   anxiously

any   ~body ~how ~one

any   ~thing ~way ~where

aorta

aparant   apparent

apart

ape

Check out
app as well

apeal   appeal

apear   appear

apel   apple

apetight   appetite

aphid

aplie   apply

aplikashun   application

aplord   applaud

apologetic

apologise

   [apologising apologised]

apology   apologies

apon   upon

apostrofee   apostrophe

apostrophe

appalling   appallingly

apparatus

apparent   apparently

apparition

appart   apart

appeal   appealingly

appear [appearing appeared]

appearance

appendix   appendicitis

appetising

appetite

applaud   applause

   [applauding applauded]

apple

application

apply [applying applied]

appolagise   apologise

appreciate   appreciation

   [appreciating appreciated]

approach   approachable

   [approaching approached]

approval		arena	
approve [approving approved]		aren't *[are not]	aunt *[family]
Aprel	April	arest	arrest
apren	apron	argew	argue
apricot		argue	
April April Fool's Day		argument argumentative	
aproch	approach	argyoumont	argument
apron		arial	aerial
apruve	approve	arithmetic	
aquarium		arival	arrival
Aquarius		arive	arrive
Arab Arabian Arabic		ark *[boat]	arc *[curve]
arange	arrange	arkade	arcade
arc *[curve]	ark *[boat]	arkangel	archangel
arcade		arkiology	archaeology
arch arches		arkitect	architect
archaeology archaeologist		Arktik	Arctic
archangel		arm armchair	
archbishop		arma	armour
archer archery		armada	
archiology	archaeology	armadillo	
architect architecture		armed forces	
archor	archer	armie	army
archway		armond	almond
Arctic Arctic Circle		armour armour-plated	
are *[we are]	our *[us]	army armies	
area		arnt	aren't *[are not]
areal	aerial		aunt *[family]

arodrome   aerodrome

arogant   arrogant

aroplane   aeroplane

arosol   aerosol

around

arow   arrow

arownd   around

arrange

   [arranging arranged]

arrangement

arrest [arresting arrested]

arrithmatic   arithmetic

arrival

arrive [arriving arrived]

arrogant   arrogantly

arrow   arrow-head

arsen   arson

arsenal

arsenic

arsk   ask

arsnick   arsenic

arson   arsonist

art

artcher   archer

arterie   artery

artery   arteries

arthritic   arthritis

artic   arctic

article

artificial   artificially

artifishall   artificial

artikal   article

artist   artistic

artrey   artery

as *[compare]   ass *[animal]

asassin   assassin

asassinate   assassinate

asc   ask

ascape   escape

ase   ace

asembly   assembly

asembul   assemble

ash   ashes   ashen

ashamed

Ashun   Asian

Asian

asist   assist

ask [asking asked]

asleep

asma   asthma

asortid   assorted

asparagus

ass *[animal]   as *[compare]

assassin   assassination

assassinate

   [assassinating assassinated]

assemble

  [assembling assembled]

assembly assemblies

assist [assisting assisted]

assistance assistant

assorted assortment

assume [assuming assumed]

Astec   Aztec

asterisk

asteroid

asthma asthmatic

astonish astonishment

astreisk   asterisk

astreoid   asteroid

astrologer

astronaut

astronomer astronomy

astronort   astronaut

asume   assume

at

atach   attach

Check out att as well

ate *[food]   eight *[number]

atempt   attempt

athlete athletic athletics

athority   authority

atic   attic

atishoo

atitude   attitude

Atlantic

atlas

atmosfere   atmosphere

atmosphere

atom atom bomb

atomic atomic energy

atract   attract

atractiv   attractive

attach [attaching attached]

attachment

attack [attacking attacked]

attempt [attempting attempted]

attend [attending attended]

attendance attendant

attention

attentive attentively

attic

attitude

attract [attracting attracted]

attraction attractive

atyshoo   atishoo

aubergine

auburn

auction auctioneer

audience

audishun   audition

audition

auditorium

auditory

auful   awful

August

aunt *[family]   ant *[insect]

  aren't *[are not]

au pair

aural aurally

Aurgast   August

aut   out

author

authorisation authority

authorise

  [authorising authorised]

autistic *[condition]

  artistic *[skill]

autism

autobiography

autograph

automatic automatically

autopilot

autumn autumnal

avacado   avocado

avacouatid   evacuated

available availability

avalanche

avaleabul   available

avaperrat   evaporate

avapourate   evaporate

avary   aviary

avelanch   avalanche

avencherus   adventurous

avenew   avenue

aventure   adventure

avenue

average

averige   average

aviary aviaries

aviashun   aviation

aviation aviator

avlanch   avalanche

avocado

avoid [avoiding avoided]

avoyd   avoid

avrage   average

awair   aware

awake

award [awarding awarded]

aware awareness

away

awayk   awake

awdiense   audience

awful awfully

awght   ought

Awgust	August	axis axes	
awkward	awkwardly	axle *[wheel]	axel *[jump]
awoke	awoken		axil *[leaf]
awr	our	ayl	ale
awt	ought	aym	aim
	out	ayt	eight *[number]
awtumn	autumn		ate *[food]
axe axes		az	as
axel *[jump]	axle *[wheel]		
axil *[leaf]			

baa [baaing]

babble [babbling babbled]

babey — baby

babminton — badminton

baboon

babul — babble

baby babyish

babysit babysitter

[babysitting babysat]

bac — back

bace — base *[bottom]

— bass *[music]

bacen — bacon

bach — batch

bachelor

back ~ache ~stroke ~wards

backhand backhanded

bacon

bacteria bacterial

bad badly badness

bad worse worst

baddy baddies

badge

badger

badminton

baffle [baffling baffled]

bag bagpipes

bagage — baggage

bage — badge

bager — badger

baggage

baggy baggier baggiest

baige — beige

baik — bake

bail *[out, cricket] bale *[bundle]

bailiff

bair — bare *[naked]

— bear *[carry, cub]

bairn

bais — base *[bottom]

bait [baited]

bak — back

bake [baking baked]

bakery

bakon — bacon

bakry — bakery

bakteria — bacteria

bal — ball *[kick]

balaclava

balad — ballad

balance

balcony

bald *[head] bawled *[cried]

— bold *[strong]

bale *[bundle] bail *[out, cricket]

balense — balance

14

balerina	ballerina
balkony	balcony
ball *[kick]	bawl *[cry]
ball	
ballad	
ballay	ballet
ballerina	
ballet	
balloon balloonist	
ballot	
ballroom	
balm	
balmy *[mild]	barmy *[mad]
baloon	balloon
balot	ballot
balune	balloon
bamboo	
bambu	bamboo
ban [banning banned]	
banana	
band *[group, stripe]	
banned *[stopped]	
bandage	
bandie	bandy
bandige	bandage
bandit	
bandy bandy-legged	

baned	band *[group, stripe]
	banned *[stopped]
baner	banner
bang [banging banged]	
bangle	
banish banishment	
banister	
banjo	
bank	
bankrupt bankruptcy	
bankwet	banquet
bannana	banana
banned *[stopped]	
band *[group, stripe]	
banner	
bannish	banish
bannister	banister
banquet	
banter	
baonnet	bayonet
baptise [baptising baptised]	
baptism	
bar *[pub]	bare *[naked]
bar *[stop]	
barage	barrage
barax	barracks

barb	barbed
barbecue	
barber	
bare *[nude]	bear *[cub]
	bear *[carry]
bare barely	
bare ~foot ~headed ~legged	
barekaid	barricade
barel	barrel
baren	baron *[noble]
	barren *[dry]
bargain [bargaining bargained]	
barge barge-pole	
bargin	bargain
baricade	barricade
barier	barrier
barister	barrister
barje	barge
bark	
barley	
barmaid barman	
barmy *[mad]	balmy *[mild]
barn	
barnacle	
barometer	
baron *[noble]	barren *[dry]
barracks	
barrel	

barren *[dry]	baron *[noble]
barricade	
barrier	
barrister	
barrow	
barscit	basket
barter [bartering bartered]	
barth	bath
bas	base *[bottom]
	bass *[music]
bascet	basket
base *[bottom]	bass *[music]
basement	
bash [bashing bashed]	
bashful bashfully	
basic basically	
basin basinful	
basis bases	
bask [basking basked]	
basket basketball	
basoon	bassoon
bass *[music]	base *[bottom]
bass-guitar bass-guitarist	
bassoon bassoonist	
baste [basting basted]	
basyn	basin
bat batsman	
batalien	battalion

batcheler	bachelor
baten	baton
bater	batter
batery	battery
bath *[tub]	
bathe *[swim] [bathing bathed]	
batik	
batrie	battery
battalion	
battel	battle
batter [battering battered]	
battery	
battle ~field ~ground	
batton	baton
battree	battery
batty battier battiest	
baul	ball *[sport, dance]
	bawl *[cry]
bawl *[cry]	ball *[kick]
bawt	bought
bay	
bayl	bale *[bundle]
	bail *[out, cricket]
bayliff	bailiff
bayonet	
bayt	bait
baything	bathing

bazaar	
bcos	because
be *[being]	bee *[insect]
beach *[sea]	beech *[tree]
beacon	
bead beady	
beaf	beef
beak beaker	
beam [beaming beamed]	
bean *[food]	been *[was]
beap	beep
bear *[cub]	bare *[naked]
beard bearded	
beast beastly	
beat [beating beaten]	
beautiful beautifully	
beauty *[lovely]	booty *[loot]
beaver	
became	
because	
beckon [beckoning beckoned]	
become [becoming became]	
becon	beckon
becos	because
becum	become
bed bed-linen	
bedlam	
Bedouin	

17

bedroom   bedside

Bedwin   Bedouin

bee *[insect]   be *[being]

beech *[tree]   beach *[sea]

beed   bead

beef   beefy

beefburger

beehive

beek   beak

beem   beam

been *[was]   bean *[food]

beep [beeping beeped]

beer

beerd   beard

beest   beast

beestro   bistro

beetle

beever   beaver

befor   before

before   beforehand

befrend   befriend

befriend [befriending befriended]

beg [begging begged]

beggar

begin [beginning began]

beginner

behave [behaving behaved]

behaviour

behead [beheading beheaded]

behed   behead

behind

behvyer   behaviour

beige

being

bekame   became

bekause   because

bekon   beckon

bel   bell

belated   belatedly

belch [belching belched]

beleif   belief

beleive   believe

belfry   belfries

belief

believe   believable

 [believing believed]

belive   believe

bell   bell-ringing

bellow *[yell]   below *[under]

bellows

belly   bellyache

belly-button   belly-flop

belong [belonging belonged]

belongings

below *[under]   bellow *[yell]

belt

bench   benches

bend [bending bent]

beneath

beneeth   beneath

benefit

bent

berbul   burble

berd   bird

berden   burden

bereaved   bereavement

bereeved   bereaved

beret *[hat]   berry *[fruit]

                   bury *[cover]

Check out bur as well

berger   burger

berglar   burglar

bergul   burgle

berial   burial

berly   burly

bern   burn

bernt   burnt

berry *[fruit]   beret *[hat]

                   bury *[cover]

berserk

berst   burst

berth *[bunk]   birth *[born]

bery   berry *[fruit]

                   bury *[cover]

beryed   buried

beseige   besiege

beside *[at the side]

besides *[apart from]

besiege [besieging besieged]

besotted

best

bet [betting betted bet]

betray [betraying betrayed]

better

between

beuteful   beautiful

beware

bewicht   bewitched

bewilder   bewilderment
   [bewildering bewildered]

bewitch [bewitching bewitched]

beyond

bhaji

bi   by *[near]

                   buy *[shop]

                   bye *[farewell]

biannual

bias   biased   biases

bib

Bible   biblical

biceps

bich   bitch

bicker [bickering bickered]

bicos   because

bicycle

bid [bidding bid]

Check out
be as well

bifour   before

big   bigger   biggest

bigan   began

biger   bigger

bigun   begun

bihave   behave

bihavior   behaviour

bihind   behind

bike

biker *[cyclist]   bicker *[row]

bikini

bil   bill

bilated   belated

bilberry   bilberries

bild   billed *[invoiced]

     build *[construct]

bilding   building

bilevabul   believable

bilingual

bilion   billion

bill

billed *[pay]   build *[house]

billiards

billion   billionaire

billy goat

biloved   beloved

bilow   below

bilt   built

bin *[box]   been *[was]

bind   binder   binding

bineath   beneath

binge

bingo

binoculars

biodegradable

biografer   biographer

biographer   biography

biological

biologist   biology

bipass   bypass

birch   birches

bird   bird-brained

birdbath   birdseed

birden   burden

birdie

bird's-eye view

birger   burger

birgler	burglar	bizee	busy
birgul	burgle	bizness	business
birnt	burnt	blab [blabbing blabbed]	
Biro™		black ~bird ~board	
birth birthday		black ~currant ~out ~smith	
biscit	biscuit	Black Death	
biscuit		blackberry blackberries	
biseige	besiege	bladder	
biseps	biceps	blade	
bishop		blader *[skater] bladder *[urine]	
biside	beside	blaid	blade
biskit	biscuit	blaim	blame
bison		blak	black
bistro		blame blameless	
bisycul	bicycle	blank blankly	
bit		blanket	
bitch bitchy		blankit	blanket
bite *[teeth] byte *[data]		blare [blaring blared]	
[biting bit bitten]		blarst	blast
bite-size bite-sized		blast blast-off	
bitray	betray	blaze [blazing blazed]	
bitter bitterly		blazer	
bitterness		bleach	
bitween	between	bleak bleakly bleakness	
biware	beware	bleat [bleating bleated]	
biwilder	bewilder	bleech	bleach
biy	buy	bleed [bleeding bled]	
biyond	beyond	bleek	bleak

bleep [bleeping bleeped]

bleet   bleat

blend

bler   blur

blert   blurt

bless [blessing blessed]

blew *[wind]   blue *[colour]

blind   blindly   blindness

blindfold   blind-man's-buff

blink [blinking blinked]

blip

bliss   blissful   blissfully

blister

Blitz [the]

blizzard

blo   blow

bloat [bloating bloated]

blob

bloch   blotch

blochy   blotchy

block [blocking blocked]

blockade

blockage

blod   blood

blog [blogging blogged]

bloke

blonde

blong   belong

blood   ~curdling ~hound

blood   ~shed ~shot ~stain

bloodthirsty

bloody

bloom [blooming bloomed]

blossom [blossoming blossomed]

blot [blotting blotted]

blotch   blotches   blotchy

blote   bloat

blouse

blow [blowing blew blown]

blubber   blubbery

blud   blood

blue *[colour]   blew *[wind]

bluebell   bluebottle

bluff [bluffing bluffed]

bluish

blume   bloom

blunder [blundering blundered]

blunt   bluntly   bluntness

blur [blurring blurred]

blurt [blurting blurted]

blush [blushing blushed]

bluwe   blue

blynd   blind

boa

boar *[pig]   bore *[dull]

board *[wood]   bored *[dull]

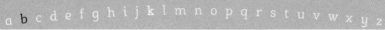

board [boarding boarded]

boast   boastful

boat   boating

bob   bobsleigh

bobble

bobul   bobble

boch   botch

body   bodies

bog   boggy

bogel   boggle

boggle [boggling boggled]

boggy

bogus

boil [boiling boiled]

boiler

boisterous   boisterously

bok   book

bolard   bollard

bold *[strong]   bald *[head]

                         bowled *[sport]

boldly

boler   bowler

bolinase   bolognaise

bollard

bolled   bald *[head]

                         bold *[strong]

                         bowled *[sport]

bolognaise [spaghetti]

bolshy

bolt [bolting bolted]

bom   bomb

bomb   bomb-disposal

bomb   ~shell ~site

bombard

   [bombarding bombarded]

bomber

bommer   bomber

bone

bonfire

Bonfire Night

bonkers

bonnet

bonus   bonuses

bony   bonier   boniest

booby   booby-prize

book   ~case ~shelf ~shop

bookay   bouquet

boom [booming boomed]

boomerang

boost [boosting boosted]

booster

boot

bootee *[shoe]   booty *[loot]

booteek   boutique

booth

booty *[loot]   bootee *[shoe]

borbul	bauble
border	borderline
bordom	boredom
bordor	border
bore *[dull]	boar *[pig]
bored *[dull]	board *[wood]
boreding	boarding
boredom	
born *[birth]	
borne *[carried]	
borrow [borrowing borrowed]	
bort	bought
bosom	
boss bossy	
bost	boast
botanist botany	
botch [botching botched]	
bote	boat
botem	bottom
both	
bother [bothering bothered]	
botom	bottom
bottle bottle-feed	
bottom bottomless	
botul	bottle
botum	bottom
bough *[branch]	bow *[bend]
bought *[buy]	brought *[bring]

boukay	bouquet
boulder *[rock]	bolder *[braver]
bounce [bouncing bounced]	
bouncy bouncier	
bound [bounding bounded]	
boundary boundaries	
bounse	bounce
bow *[bend]	bough *[branch]
bow *[arrow, knot]	
bow [bowing bowed]	
bowel *[tummy]	
bowl *[dish]	
bowl *[action] [bowling bowled]	
bowler	
bowndree	boundary
bownse	bounce
box boxes	
boxer	
Boxing Day	
boy *[male]	buoy *[float]
boycott	
boyfriend boyhood	
boyish	
boyl	boil
Boy Scout	
boystrus	boisterous
bra bras	
brace [bracing braced]	

bracelet

bracken

bracket

brag [bragging bragged]

braid *[hair]   brayed *[ass]

braille

brain   brainwave

brainy   brainier   brainiest

brake *[slow]   break *[snap]

brake [braking braked]

braket   bracket

bramble

bran *[cereal]   brain *[mind]

branch   branches

brand   brand-new

brandish [brandishing brandished]

brane   brain

brar   bra

bras *[underwear] brass *[metal]

braselet   bracelet

brash

brass   brassy

brat   brattish   brattishly

braul   brawl

brave   braver   bravest

bravery

brawd   broad

brawl

brawt   brought

bray [braying brayed]

braynee   brainy

bread *[food]   breed *[type]

break *[snap]   brake *[slow]

break [breaking broke broken]

break   ~neck ~through

breakfast

breast   breastbone

breath   breathy

breathe [breathing breathed]

breathless   breathlessly

breathtaking

breaze   breeze

brecfst   breakfast

bred *[animal]   bread *[food]

                    breed *[type]

breed   breeder   breeding

breef   brief

breethe   breathe

breeze   breezy

breif   brief

brekfast   breakfast

brest   breast

breth   breath *[air]

                    breathe

                    *[in and out]

brethtaking   breathtaking

brew [brewing brewed]

brewed *[tea]   brood *[kids]

brewery   breweries

bribe [bribing bribed]

bribery

brick

bridal *[wedding] bridle *[horse]

bride   ~groom ~smaid

bridge

bridle *[horse]

　bridal *[wedding]

brief   briefest   briefly

brieze   breeze

brigade

brige   bridge

bright   brighter   brightest

brighten [brightening brightened]

brik   brick

brilliance

brilliant   brilliantly

brim

bring [bringing brought]

brisk   briskly

bristle   bristly

Britain *[place]   Briton *[person]

brite   bright

British

Briton *[person]   Britain *[place]

Britten   Britain

broad   broader   broadest

broaden [broadening broadened]

broadly

broak   broke

broccoli

broch   brooch

brocher   brochure

brochure

brocoli   broccoli

broke   broken

brokn   broken

bronse   bronze

brontosaurus

bronze   Bronze Age

brooch   brooches

brood *[kids]   brewed *[tea]

broody   broodier   broodiest

brook

broom   broomstick

broose   bruise

broot   brute

brord   broad

brort   brought

brother   brother-in-law

brought *[bring] bought *[buy]

brow

brown

brownie *[cake]

Brownie *[club]

browse [browsing browsed]

browser

brud   brood

brue   brew

bruise [bruising bruised]

brume   broom

brunch

brunette

brush   brushes

Brussels   brussels sprouts

brutal   brutally

brute   brutish

bruther   brother

brutle   brutal

brydal   bridal *[wedding]

                 bridle *[horse]

bryde   bride

bubble [bubbling bubbled]

bubbly

bucher   butcher

buck [bucking bucked]

bucket [bucketing bucketed]

Buckingham Palace

buckle   buckles

bud [budding budded]

Buddha

Buddhism   Buddhist

buddy   buddies

budge [budging budged]

budgerigar   budgie

budget [budgeting budgeted]

Budha   Buddha

bufalo   buffalo

buffalo   buffaloes

buffay   buffet

buffet *[food]

buffet *[wind] [buffeted]

bug [bugging bugged]

bugel   bugle

bugerigar   budgerigar

buget   budget

buggy   buggies

bugle

build *[construct]   billed *[invoiced]

building

built   built-up

bujet   budget

bul   bull

bulb   bulbous

bulee   bully

bulge [bulging bulged]

bulit   bullet

bulitin   bulletin

bulj   bulge

bulk   bulky

bull   bullock

bull   ~dog ~fight ~finch

bulldoze   bulldozer

  [bulldozing bulldozed]

bullet

bulletin

bullion

bully [bullying bullied]

bully   bullies

bulrush   bulrushes

buly   bully

bumble [bumbling bumbled]

bumblebee

bumerang   boomerang

bump [bumping bumped]

bumpy   bumpier   bumpiest

bun   bunfight

bunch   bunches

bundle [bundling bundled]

bung [bunging bunged]

bungalow

bungee

bungel   bungle

bungie   bungee

bungle [bungling bungled]

bunglo   bungalow

bunjie   bungee

bunk

bunker

bunny   bunnies

Bunsen burner

bunsh   bunch

buoy *[float]   boy *[male]

burble [burbling burbled]

burch   birch

burd   bird

burden [burdening burdened]

burgeld   burgled

burger

burglar

burglary   burglaries

burgle *[rob]   bugle *[horn]

burial

burly   burlier   burliest

burn [burning burned]

burnt

burp [burping burped]

burrow *[dig]   borrow *[loan]

bursar   bursary   bursaries

burst [bursting burst]

bursurk   berserk

burth   berth *[bunk]

                  birth *[born]

bury *[cover]   berry *[fruit]

bus   buses

busel   bustle

bush   bushes

bushy   bushier   bushiest

business   businesses

business   ~man ~woman

busker   busking

bussel   bustle

bustle [bustling]

busy   busier   busiest

but *[however]   butt *[hit]

buten   button

buter   butter

butie   beauty *[lovely]

                      booty *[loot]

butiful   beautiful

butler

buton   button

butter   buttery

butter   ~cup ~fly ~scotch

buttock   buttocks

button   buttonhole

buty   beauty *[lovely]

                      booty *[loot]

buy *[shop]   bye *[goodbye]

                      by *[near]

buy [buying bought]

buzz [buzzes buzzing buzzed]

buzzard

bwuty   beauty

by *[near]   buy *[shop]

                      bye *[goodbye]

byceps   biceps

Check out
bi as well

bycicul   bicycle

bye *[goodbye]   buy *[shop]

                      by *[near]

byer   buyer

bynoculars   binoculars

bypass bypasses

 [bypassing bypassed]

byte *[data]   bite *[teeth]

cab

cabale   cable

cabbage

cabin

cable

cackle [cackling cackled]

cactus   cacti

cadge [cadging cadged]

café *[snack]   coffee *[cup]

cage

caik   cake

caim   came

cair   care

caireful   careful

cake

calcium

calculate [calculating calculated]

calculation   calculator

calendar *[date]   colander *[food]

calf *[baby cow]   calves

               calve *[give birth]

call [calling called]

calm   calmer   calmly

calorie   calories

calqulashun   calculation

calqulate   calculate

calqulator   calculator

calsium   calcium

calve *[give birth] carve *[cut]
  [calving calved]

camaflarge   camouflage

came

camel

camelion   chameleon

camera ~man

camouflage

camp ~fire ~ground ~site

campaign
  [campaigning campaigned]

camra   camera

can *[able, tin]   cane *[stick]

canal

canary   canaries

cancel [cancelling cancelled]

cancellation

cancer *[illness]

Cancer *[zodiac]

candel   candle

candle ~light ~lit ~stick

candy ~floss

cane

canibal   cannibal

cannibal   cannibalism

cannon   cannonball

cannot

canoe [canoeing canoed]

cansel · cancel
canser · cancer *[illness]
· Cancer *[zodiac]
can't *[cannot]
canter [cantering cantered]
canue · canoe
canvas
canyon
cap *[hat, top] · cape *[cloak, land]
capable
capcher · capture
capillary capillaries
capital
Capricorn
capshun · caption
capsize [capsizing capsized]
capsule
captain
capten · captain
capter · captor
caption
captive captivity
capture
[capturing captured]
car carsick
caracter · character
caramel
carat *[gold] · carrot *[food]

caravan caravanning
carbohydrate
carbon
carbord · cardboard
carcass carcasses
card cardboard
cardigan
cardinal
care carefree
caree · carry
career *[job] · carrier *[carries]
careful carefully
careless carelessly
carelessness
caretaker caretaking
cargo cargoes
Caribbean
carier · career *[job]
· carrier *[carries]
carm · calm
carnation
carnival
carnivore carnivorous
carol carol-singing
carot · carat *[gold]
· carrot *[food]
carpenter carpentry
carpet [carpeting carpeted]

31

carriage ~way

carrige   carriage

carrot *[food]   carat *[gold]

carry [carrying carried]

carsel   castle

cart *[transport] kart *[go-kart]

cart   ~horse ~load ~wheel

carten   carton

carton *[box]

cartoon cartoonist

cartridge

cartune   cartoon

carve *[cut]   calve *[give birth]
  [carving carved]

carving

caryon   carrion

case [casing cased]

casel   castle

caset   cassette

cash *[money]   catch *[ball]

casheltee   casualty

cashew

cashier

cashmere

cashoe   cashew

casino

casserole   [casseroled]

cassette

cast castaway

caster *[sugar]   castor *[oil,
                        wheel]

castle

casual casually

casualty casualties

casum   chasm

cat

catacomb catacombs

catalogue catalogues

catapult [catapulting catapulted]

catar   catarrh

catarrh

catastrofee   catastrophe

catastrophe catastrophic

catch [catching caught]

category categories

catekoom   catacomb

catel   cattle

catelog   catalogue

catepolt   catapult

cater [catering catered]

caterpillar

cathedral

Catholic Catholicism

catkin

catnap [catnapping catnapped]

cattle

caturpillar   caterpillar

caught *[ball]   court *[law]

cauldron

cauliflower

cause [causing caused]

caushun   caution

caushus   cautious

caution [cautioning cautioned]

cautious   cautiously

cavalry

cave   caveman

cavity   cavities

cavurn   cavern

caw *[crow]   core *[centre]
            corps *[army]

cawling   calling

cawps   corpse

cayg   cage

caym   came

cease *[stop]   seize *[grab]

Check out
se as well

ceaseless   ceaselessly

cedate   sedate

ceeje   siege

ceiling *[roof]   sealing
            *[fastening]

celebrate   celebration
  [celebrating celebrated]

celebrity   celebrities

celery

cell *[prison]   sell *[shop]

cellabration   celebration

cellar *[room]   seller *[sales
                    person]

cello   cellist

Celsius

Celt   Celtic

cement [cementing cemented]

cemetery   cemeteries

cene   scene *[theatre]
        seen *[eyes]

cenile   senile

census

cent *[money]   scent *[smell]
                sent *[away]

centaur

centenary

center   centre

centigrade

centimetre

centipede

centir   centre

central

centre [centring centred]

33

centry	sentry	certificate	
centurion		certsy	curtsy
century centuries		cerve	curve
cenyer	senior	cesspit	
cep	keep	cew	cue *[signal]
ceramic			queue *[line]
cerb	curb *[stop]	chain [chaining chained]	
	kerb *[edge]	chair	
cercul	circle	chaist	chased
cercus	circus	chalet	
cereal *[grain]	serial *[sequence]	chalinge	challenge
cerebral palsy		chalk chalky	
ceremonial		challenge [challenging challenged]	
ceremony ceremonies		chamber	
cerf	serf *[slave]	chameleon	
	surf *[sea]	champagne	campaign
cerfew	curfew	*[wine]	*[activity]
cerial	cereal *[grain]	champion championship	
	serial *[sequence]	chance chances chancy	
cerialise	serialise	chandelier	
cerkit	circuit	chane	chain
cername	surname	change [changing changed]	
cerse	curse	changeable	
cersor	cursor	chanj	change
certain *[sure]	curtain *[window]	channel [channelling]	
certainty certainties		Channel [the English]	
certen	certain *[sure]	chanse	chance
	curtain *[window]	chant [chanting chanted]	

chaos   chaotic

chap

chapati

chapel   chaplain

chaplin   chaplain

chapter

chapul   chapel

character   characteristic

charade

charcoal

chare   chair

charge [charging charged]

chariot   charioteer

charitable

charity   charities

charm [charming charmed]

charnce   chance

charnt   chant

chart [charting charted]

charter flight

chase [chasing chased]

chasm   chasms

chat [chatting chatted]

chateau

chatter [chattering chattered]

chatty   chattier

chauffeur

chaw   chore

cheap *[money]   cheep *[bird]

cheap   cheaper   cheaply

cheat [cheating cheated]

check *[inspect]   cheque *[money]
  [checking checked]

checkmate

Cheddar cheese

cheef   chief

cheeften   chieftain

cheek

cheeky   cheekier   cheekiest

cheep *[bird]   cheap *[money]

cheepen   cheapen

cheer [cheering cheered]

cheerful   cheerfully

cheerfulness

cheese   ~burger ~cake

cheesy   cheesier   cheesiest

cheetah

chef *[cook]   chief *[boss]

cheir   chair

chello   cello

chemical   chemically

chemist   chemistry

cheque *[money]   check *[inspect]

cherch   church

chere   chair

cheree   cherry

cherish [cherishes]

[cherishing cherished]

chern   churn

cherry   cherries

cherub   cherubic

chess   chessboard

chest   chesty

chestnut

chew [chewing chewed]

chews *[food]   choose *[pick]

chewy   chewier   chewiest

chick

chicken   chickenpox

chickpea

chief   chiefs   chiefly

chieftain

chier   cheer

chiffon

chilblain

child   children   childish

chill [chilling chilled]

chilli *[food]   chillis

chilly *[cold]   chillier

chime [chiming chimed]

chimney   chimneys

chimp   chimpanzee

chin   chinless

china *[cup]   China *[place]

chinchilla

Chinese

chink

chip [chipping chipped]

chipmunk

chipolata

chirp [chirping chirped]

chirpy   chirpier   chirpiest

chisel [chiselling chiselled]

chivalry   chivalrous

chloride

chlorine

chlorophyll

chocerlit   chocolate

chocolate

chofer   chauffeur

choice

choir

choke [choking choked]

cholera

cholesterol

choose *[pick]   chews *[food]

[choosing chose chosen]

choosy   choosier   choosiest

chop [chopping chopped]

chopsticks

choppy   choppier   choppiest

choral

chord *[music]   cord *[rope]

chore

chork   chalk

chortle [chortling chortled]

chorus   choruses

choys   choice

Christ

christal   crystal

christen [christening christened]

Christian   Christianity

Christmas

chriy   try

chrome

chromosome

chronic

chronicle

chronological

chrysalis   chrysalises

chrysanthemum

chrystallise   crystallise

chubby   chubbier   chubbiest

chuck [chucking chucked]

chuckle [chuckling chuckled]

chue   chew

chug [chugging chugged]

chum   chummy   chummier

chunk   chunky   chunkier

church   churches

churn [churning churned]

churp   chirp

chuse   choose

chute *[slide]   shoot *[target]

chyna   china

cianide   cyanide

cichin   kitchen

ciclist   cyclist

ciclone   cyclone

cicul   cycle

cider

ciense   science

cientific   scientific

cigar   cigarette

cignet   cygnet *[swan]
                signet *[ring]

cilindar   cylinder

cimbal   cymbal *[music]
                symbol *[sign]

cinder

cinema

cinus   sinus

circit   circuit

circle

circuit

circular

circulate   circulation
  [circulating circulated]

circumference

circumstance

circus   circuses

cissors   scissors

Check out si as well

cissy   cissies

cist   cyst

citadel

cite *[quote]   sight *[seeing]

  [citing cited]   site *[place]

citee   city

citizen   citizenship

citrus

city   cities

civil   civilian

civilisation

civilise [civilising civilised]

clad

claim [claiming claimed]

clairvoyant

clam

clamber [clambering clambered]

clame   claim

clammy   clammier

clamp [clamping clamped]

clan

clang [clanging clanged]

clank [clanking clanked]

clap [clapping clapped]

clarinet   clarinettist

clarss   class

clash [clashes clashing clashed]

clasik   classic

clasp [clasping clasped]

class   classes

class   ~room ~work

classic   classical

clatter [clattering clattered]

clause *[part]   claws *[animal]

claustrophobia

claustrophobic

claw [clawing clawed]

claws *[animal]   clause *[part]

clay

clean [cleaning cleaned]

cleanliness   cleanly

cleanse [cleansing cleansed]

clear [clearing cleared]

clear   clearly

cleen   clean

cleer   clear

cleeshay   cliché

clementine

clench [clenching clenched]

38

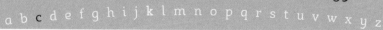

clense   cleanse

clergy

clever   cleverer   cleverest

cleverly   cleverness

clew   clue

cliché

client

cliff   cliffhanger

clik   click

clim   climb

climate   climatic

climax   climaxes

climb [climbing climbed]

climed   climbed

climing   climbing

cling [clinging clung]

clinic

clink [clinking clinked]

clip [clipping clipped]

cloak   cloakroom

clobber [clobbering clobbered]

clock   clockwork

clockwatch   [clockwatches]

clog [clogged]

cloke   cloak

clone

clorafill   chlorophyll

clore   claw

cloride   chloride

clorinate   chlorinate

clorine   chlorine

clorofill   chlorophyll

clors   clause *[part]

           claws *[animal]

clorstrofobia   claustrophobia

close [closing closed]

close   closer   closest

closely   closeness

closet

clot [clotting clotted]

cloth *[material]

clothe *[put clothes on]

clothes   clothing

cloud   cloudless

cloudy   cloudier   cloudiest

clout [clouting clouted]

clove

clover

clowd   cloud

clown   clownish

clowt   clout

club [clubbing clubbed]

cluch   clutch

cluck [clucking clucked]

clue   clueless

clump [clumping clumped]

clumpy clumpier clumpiest

clumsy clumsier clumsiest

clunk [clunking clunked]

clurgy   clergy

cluster [clustering clustered]

clutch clutches

  [clutching clutched]

clutter [cluttering cluttered]

clyent   client

clyme   climb

coach coaches

  [coaching coached]

coal coalmine

coarse coarsely

coast ~guard ~line

coastal

coat

cobble cobblestone

  [cobbling cobbled]

cobra

cobweb

Coca Cola™

coch   coach

cock cock-a-doodle-doo

cockatoo

cockerel

cockney

cockpit

cockroach cockroaches

cocky cockier cockiest

cocoa

coco   cocoa

coconut

cocoon [cocooning cocooned]

cocune   cocoon

cod

code

coed   could

coff   cough

coffee *[cup]   café *[snack]

coffin

cohort

coil [coiling coiled]

coin [coining coined]

coincidence

cokatoo   cockatoo

cola *[drink]   collar *[neck]

colander *[food] calendar *[time]

colaps   collapse

cold colder coldest

coldly coldness

cole   coal

coleeg   colleague

coler   collar *[neck]

              colour *[red]

colera   cholera

colerbone	collarbone
colerful	colourful
coleslaw	
colesterol	cholesterol
colide	collide
colige	college
collage	
collapse	collapsible
[collapsing collapsed]	
collar	collarbone
collarj	collage
colleague	
collecshun	collection
collect	collector
[collecting collected]	
collection	
college	
collide [colliding collided]	
colliflower	cauliflower
collision	
colloquial	
collum	column
colon	
colonel *[army]	kernel *[seed]
colony	colonies
coloqueal	colloquial
colour	colourless
colourful	colourfully

column	
coma *[sleep]	comma *[text]
comando	commando
comb	
combat	
combine	combination
[combining combined]	
come [coming came]	
comedian	comedy comedies
comeing	coming
comemorate	commemorate
comen	common
comense	commence
coment	comment
comentry	commentary
comershal	commercial
comet *[sky]	commit *[to do]
comforball	comfortable
comfort [comforting comforted]	
comfortable	comfortably
comfy	
comic	comical
comidian	comedian
coming	
comit	comet *[sky]
	commit *[to do]
comitee	committee
comma *[text]	coma *[sleep]

command   commander
  [commanding commanded]
commando
commemorate
commence
  [commencing commenced]
comment   commentator
  [commenting commented]
commentary   commentaries
commer   comma
commercial   commercially
commic   comic
commit *[to do]   comet *[sky]
commit   commitment
  [committing committed]
committee
common   commonly
Commonwealth Games
commotion
communicate
  [communicating communicated]
communication
communism   communist
community   communities
commute   commuter
  [commuting commuted]
comon   common
comoshun   commotion

compact
compair   compare
companion
company   companies
companyon   companion
compare   comparison
  [comparing compared]
compartment
compashun   compassion
compass   compasses
compassion   compassionate
compeet   compete
compensate   compensation
  [compensating compensated]
compete   competitor
  [competing competed]
competent   competently
competition   competitive
compitishun   competition
complain   complaint
  [complaining complained]
complane   complain
compleks   complex
complekshun   complexion
complete   completely
  [completing completed]
complex
complexion

42

complicate   complication

[complicating complicated]

compliment   complimentary

compose [composing composed]

compost

compound

comprehend

[comprehending comprehended]

comprehension

  comprehensive

comprihenshun comprehension

compulsion   compulsive

compulsory

computer

comunicate   communicate

comunism   communism

comunitee   community

comute   commute

con [conning conned]

concave

conceal [concealing concealed]

conceit   [conceited]

concensus   consensus

concentrate   concentration

  [concentrating concentrated]

concepshun   conception

concept

conception

concequense   consequence

concern [concerning concerned]

concert

concienshus   conscientious

concious   conscious

concise   concisely

concist   consist

concistency   consistency

conclewd   conclude

conclude   conclusion

  [concluding concluded]

concoct   concoction

  [concocting concocted]

concrete

concussed   concussion

condem   condemn

condemn   condemnation

  [condemning condemned]

condense   condensation

  [condensing condensed]

condishun   condition

condition   conditional

conditioner

conduct   conductor

  [conducting conducted]

cone

conference

conferm   confirm

43

confess confession
[confessing confessed]
confest   confessed
confetti
confide confidence
[confiding confided]
confident confidently
confidential confidentially
confine [confined]
confirm confirmation
[confirming confirmed]
confiscate confiscation
[confiscating confiscated]
conflict
confrence   conference
confront confrontation
[confronting confronted]
confuse confusion
[confusing confused]
confyde   confide
congrachulate congratulate
congratulate
[congratulating congratulated]
congratulations
conical
conifer coniferous
conjer   conjure
conjunction

conjure conjuror
[conjuring conjured]
conkave   concave
conker *[nut]   conquer *[win]
conkrete   concrete
conkussed   concussed
conkwest   conquest
connect connection
[connecting connected]
conquer *[win]   conker *[nut]
conqueror conquest
conscience
conscientious
conscientiously
conscious consciously
conseat   conceit
consecutive consecutively
conseel   conceal
conseive   conceive
consensus
consent [consenting consented]
consentrashun concentration
consentrate concentrate
consept   concept
consequence
consern   concern
consert   concert
conservation

44

conservative

conservatory

conserve [conserving conserved]

conshense   conscience

conshienshus   conscientious

conshus   conscious

consider   considerable

  [considering considered]

considerate   consideration

consise   concise

consist [consisting consisted]

consistent   consistently

consolation prize

console [consoling consoled]

consonant

conspiracy   conspiracies

constable

constant

constellation

constipated   constipation

construcshun   construction

construct   construction

  [constructing constructed]

constructive   constructively

consult   consultant

  [consulting consulted]

consume   consumer

  [consuming consumed]

consurlashun   consolation

consurvashun   conservation

consurvativ   conservative

consurvatory   conservatory

consyoum   consume

contact [contacting contacted]

contagious

contain   container

  [containing contained]

contajus   contagious

contaminate   contamination

  [contaminating contaminated]

contane   contain

contemplate   contemplation

  [contemplating contemplated]

contemporary

  contemporaries

contempt

content   contentment

contest   contestant

  [contesting contested]

context

continent *[land mass]

Continent *[the]

continual   continually

continuation

continue   continuity

  [continuing continued]

continuous   continuously

contour

contract   contractor
  [contracting contracted]

contradict   contradiction
  [contradicting contradicted]

contraption

contrary

contrast [contrasting contrasted]

contredict   contradict

contrery   contrary

contribute   contributor
  [contributing contributed]

contribution

control   controllable
  [controlling controlled]

controversy   controversial

convay   convey

convayer belt   conveyor belt

convecshun   convection

convection   convector

conveks   convex

convenient   conveniently

convent

conversation

conversion

convert   convertible
  [converting converted]

convex

convey [conveying conveyed]

conveyor belt

convict   conviction
  [convicting convicted]

convince [convincing convinced]

convinient   convenient

convinse   convince

convoy

convulse [convulsed]

convulsion

convursashun   conversation

convurshun   conversion

convurt   convert

cood   could

cook   cooker
  [cooking cooked]

cookery

cool   cooler   coolest

coolly

co-operate   co-operation
  [co-operating co-operated]

co-operative

co-operatively

co-ordinashun   co-ordination

co-ordinate   co-ordinator
  [co-ordinating co-ordinated]

co-ordination

cop *[get] [copping copped]

cope *[deal with] [coping coped]

copie   copy

co-pilot

copper

copy   copies [copying copied]

coral *[sea]   choral *[sing]

Coran   Koran

cord *[rope]   chord *[music]

corduroy

core *[centre]   caw *[crow]

                       corps *[army]

corel   choral *[sing]

               coral *[sea]

corespond   correspond

corght   caught *[ball]

               court *[law]

corige   courage

corjet   courgette

cork   corkscrew

corldron   cauldron

corled   called

cormorant

corn   corn-on-the-cob

corner

cornet

corny

corode   corrode

corporal

corprel   corporal

corps *[army]

corpse *[body]

corral *[pen]   coral *[sea]

correct   correction
  [correcting corrected]

correspond   correspondence
  [corresponding corresponded]

corridor

corroad   corrode

corrode [corroding corroded]

corrugated iron

cors   cause *[reason]
              course *[order,
                       path]

corse   cause *[reason]
              coarse *[rough]
              course *[order,
                       path]

corshun   caution

cort   caught *[ball]
              court *[law]

cortier   courtier

cortmarshall   court-martial

coschume   costume

cosee   cosy

cosmetic

cosmonaut

cost *[value]   coast *[sea]

cost   costly

coste   coast

costume

cosy   cosier   cosiest

cot *[bed]   coat *[clothing]

coton   cotton

cottage

cotton

couch   couches

cough

could   couldn't [could not]

counsellor

count   counter

  [counting counted]

countess

country   countries

county   counties

couple

couplet

courage

courageous   courageously

courd   cord *[rope]

                 chord *[music]

courgette

courier

course *[meal]   coarse *[rough]

coursework

court *[law]   caught *[ball]

courteous   courteously

courtesy *[polite] curtsy *[bow]

court-martial

cousin

cove

cover [covering covered]

cow   ~boy ~girl ~slip

coward

cowardly   cowardice

cowch   couch

cownsel   council

                       *[assembly]

counsel *[advise]

  [counselling counselled]

cownseller   counsellor

                       *[adviser]

cownt   count

coyn   coin

cozmetic   cosmetic

cozmic   cosmic

cozmonort   cosmonaut

crab   crabby

crack [cracking cracked]

crackle [crackling crackled]

cradle [cradling cradled]

craft   craftsman

crafty   craftier   craftiest

crag   craggy

craip   crepe *[paper]
                      crêpe *[pancake]

craizee   crazy

crak   crack

crakul   crackle

cram [cramming crammed]

cramp [cramping cramped]

cranberry   cranberries

crane [craning craned]

crank [cranking cranked]

cranky   crankier   crankiest

crash *[accident]   crashes
                    crush *[squash]

crash [crashes crashing crashed]

crate *[box]

crater *[large hole]

crawl [crawling crawled]

crayon

craze   crazy   crazier

creacher   creature

creak   creaky

cream   creamy

creap   creep

crease [creasing creased]

create   creator   creation
   [creating created]

creative   creatively

creativity

creature

crèche

crecher   creature

credit [credited]

creem   cream

creep   creeper   creepy
   [creeping crept]

creese   crease

cremation   crematorium

crepe *[paper]

crêpe *[pancake]

crepey   creepy

crept

crescent

cress

cressent   crescent

crevasse *[ice]

crevice *[crack]

crew

criashun   creation

criate   create

criativ   creative

crib

cricket   cricketer

crie   cry

cried

crikit   cricket

crime

criminal

crimson

cringe [cringing cringed]

crinj   cringe

crinkle   crinkly

cript   crypt

crisis   crises

crisp   crispy   crispier

crissen   christen

Crist   Christ

cristal   crystal

criteria

critic   critical   critically

criticise   criticism

    [criticising criticised]

critisize   criticise

croak   croaky   croakier

    [croaking croaked]

crock   crockery

crocodile

crocus   crocuses

crokay   croquet

croke   croak

crokodile   crocodile

crokus   crocus

crome   chrome

crook   crooked

crop [cropping cropped]

croquet

crorl   crawl

cross   crosser   crossly

cross   ~roads ~word

crouch [crouching crouched]

croud   crowd

crow [crowing crowed]

crowch   crouch

crowd *[people]

crowed *[cockerel]

crowkay   croquet

crown [crowning crowned]

cruch   crutch

crucified   crucifix

crude   crudely

crue   crew

cruel   crueller

cruelly   cruelty

cruise *[trip]   crews *[teams]

crumb   crumbly

crumble *[break]

    [crumbling crumbled]

crumple *[crease] [crumpled]

crunch   crunchy   crunchier

    [crunching crunched]

crusade   crusader

crush [crushing crushed]

crust   crusty

crutch   crutches

cry   cries

cry [cries crying cried]

crysalis   chrysalis

crysanthemum

                    chrysanthemum

crystal

cryticysum   criticism

cub

cube   cuboid

cubicle

cubord   cupboard

cuckoo

cucumber

cud

cuddle   cuddly [cuddling cuddled]

cue *[signal]   queue *[line]

cuff   cufflink

culcher   culture

cule   cool

cull [culling culled]

culla   colour

culprit

cultivate   cultivator

  [cultivating cultivated]

cultivation

culture   cultural

cum   come

cumfertabul   comfortable

cumfort   comfort

cumfy   comfy

cumpanee   company

cumpass   compass

cunning   cunningly

cuntree   country

cup   cupful   cuppa

cupboard

Cupid

cuple   couple

curb *[stop]   kerb *[edge]

cure [curing cured]

curensy   currency

curent   currant *[fruit]

                     current *[flow,

                           now]

curfew

curier   courier

curiosity

curious   curiously

curl [curling curled]

curly   curlier

currage   courage

currant *[fruit]   current *[flow,

                           now]

currency   currencies

current *[flow,   currant *[fruit]
           now]

current   currently

curriculum

curry   curries

curse [cursing cursed]

cursive

cursor

curtain *[net]   certain *[sure]

curtificate   certificate

curtsy *[bow]   courtesy

                        *[polite]

curve [curving curved]

cury   curry

cushion

cusin   cousin

custard

custody

custom   customer

cut *[with a knife]   cutter
  [cutting cut]

cute *[sweet] cuter   cutest

cutlery

cuver   cover

cyanide

cyberspace

cycle [cycling cycled]

cyclist

cyclone   cyclonic

cygnet *[swan]   signet *[ring]

cylinder   cylindrical

cymbal *[music]   symbol *[sign]

cymbolic   symbolic

cynonim   synonym

cyringe   syringe

cyrup   syrup

cystem   system

cyte   sight

czar   czarina

Check out
sy as well

D-Day

dab [dabbing dabbed]

dabble [dabbling dabbled]

dabel   dabble

Dachshund

dad   daddy   daddies

daffodil

daft   dafter   daftest

dagger

daily

dair   dare

dairy *[milk]   diary *[book]

daisy   daisies

Dalmashun   Dalmatian

Dalmatian

dam *[water]   damn *[curse]

damage [damaging damaged]

dame

damige   damage

damn *[curse]   dam *[water]
   [damning damned]

damp   dampness

dampen [dampening dampened]

damson

dance [dancing danced]

dandelion

dandruff

dandylion   dandelion

danger   dangerous

dangerously

dangle [dangling dangled]

dangros   dangerous

danjer   danger

dank

dans   dance

dapple [dappling dappled]

dare [daring dared]

darey   dairy

dark   darkly   darkness

darken [darkening darkened]

darling

darn [darning darned]

dart [darting darted]

dash   dashes [dashing dashed]

data   database

date [dating dated]

daughter

daun   dawn

dauter   daughter

dawdle   dawdler
  [dawdling dawdled]

dawn [dawning dawned]

daxhound   Dachshund

day   ~break ~dream ~light

dayity   deity

dayly   daily

days *[dates]   daze *[stun]

dayt   date

daze *[stun]   days *[dates]

dazzle [dazzling dazzled]

dead *[not alive]   deed *[action]

deaden [deadening deadened]

deadly   deadlier

deaf   deafness

deafen [deafening deafened]

deafeningly

deal [dealing dealt]

dealer   dealership

dealt

dear *[loved]   deer *[animal]

dearest   dearly

death   deathly

debait   debate

debatable

debate [debating debated]

debt   debtor

decade   decayed
   *[10 years]   *[rotted]

decarate   decorate

decay [decaying decayed]

deceit   deceitful

deceitfully   deceitfulness

deceive [deceiving deceived]

December

decent *[good]   descent *[down]

decently

deception

deceptive   deceptively

decibel

decide [deciding decided]

decidedly

deciduous

decimal

decipher [deciphering deciphered]

decision

deck [decking decked]

declaration

declare [declaring declared]

decline [declining declined]

decode [decoding decoded]

decomposed

decorate   decorator
   [decorating decorated]

decoration

decorative   decoratively

decoy

decrativ   decorative

decrease   decreasingly
   [decreasing decreased]

decree *[law]   degree *[uni]

ded   dead *[not alive]

        deed *[action]

54

dedicate   dedication
[dedicating dedicated]
deduct   deduction
[deducting deducted]
deed *[action]   dead *[not alive]
deel   deal
deep   deeply
deepen [deepening deepened]
deepfreeze   deep-frozen
deer *[animal]   dear *[loved]
deezel   diesel
def   deaf
defeat [defeating deafeated]
defect
defence   defenceless
defend   defendant
[defending defended]
defens   defence
defensive   defensively
deffen   deafen
defiant   defiantly
define [defining defined]
definetly   definitely
definishun   definition
definite   definitely
definition
deform [deformed]
deformity   deformities

defrost [defrosting defrosted]
defuse [defusing defused]
defy [defies defying defied]
degree *[uni]   decree *[law]
dehydrate [dehydrated]
de-ice [de-icing de-iced]
deity   deities
deject [dejected]   dejection
dek   deck
dekorate   decorate
delay [delaying delayed]
delete   deletion [deleting deleted]
deliberate   deliberately
[deliberating deliberated]
delicacy   delicacies
delicate   delicately
delicatessen
delicious   deliciously
delight [delighting delighted]
delightful   delightfully
delinquent   delinquency
delishus   delicious
deliver   deliverer
[delivering delivered]
delivery   deliveries
delt   dealt
deluge [deluged]
demand [demanding demanded]

demented   dementia

demerara

demist [demisting demisted]

demo

democratic   democratically

demolish [demolishes]

[demolishing demolished]

demolition

demon   demonic

demonstrate   demonstration

[demonstrating demonstrated]

demoralise

[demoralising demoralised]

den

dencher   denture

denial

denim

denomination   denominator

dense *[thick]   dents *[dips]

density

dent [denting dented]

dental

dentist   denture

deny [denies denying denied]

denyal   denial

deodorant

depart   departure

[departing departed]

department

depend   dependable

[depending depended]

dependence   dependent

depict [depicting depicted]

depo   depot

deport [deporting deported]

deportation

deposit

depot

depress   depression

[depressing depressed]

deprive   deprivation

[depriving deprived]

depth

deputy

derail [derailing derailed]

derelict

dert   dirt

descant

descend   descendant

[descending descended]

descent *[down]   decent *[good]

descrete   discreet

describe [describing described]

description   descriptive

deseet   deceit

Desember   December

desent   decent

desert *[sand]   dessert *[food]

desert *[leave]   desertion

deserve   deservedly
  [deserving deserved]

desibell   decibel

deside   decide

desifer   decipher

design   designer
  [designing designed]

desimal   decimal

desirable

desire [desiring desired]

desk

despair   despairingly
  [despairing despaired]

desperashun   desperation

desperate   desperately

desperation

despise [despising despised]

despite

deposit [depositing deposited]

despute   dispute

dessend   descend

dessent   decent *[good]

    descent *[down]

dessert *[food]   desert *[sand]

    desert *[leave]

destination

destiny   [destined]

destroy   destroyer
  [destroying destroyed]

destruction

destructive   destructively

det   debt

detail [detailing detailed]

detain [detaining detained]

detect [detecting detected]

detectable   detection

detector   detective

detention

deter   deterrant
  [deterring deterred]

detergent

deteriate   deteriorate

deteriorate   deterioration
  [deteriorating deteriorated]

determination

determine   determined

detest   detestable
  [detesting detested]

deth   death

detonate   detonator
  [detonating detonated]

detour

deuce

devastate   devastation
   [devastating devastated]
develop   development
   [developing developed]
device *[thing]   devise *[invent]
devide   divide
devil
devious   deviously
devise *[invent]   device *[thing]
devorse   divorce
devoshun   devotion
devote [devoting devoted]
devotion
devour [devouring devoured]
devout   devoutly
devyce   device *[thing]
                   devise *[invent]
dew *[drops]   Jew *[religion]
               due *[owing]
dewet   duet
dewy
diabetes   diabetic
diafram   diaphragm
diagnose [diagnosed]
diagnosis   diagnoses
diagonal   diagonally
diagram
dial [dialling dialled]

dialect
dialogue
diameter
diamond
diaphragm
diar   dire *[bad]
                   dear *[loved]
                   deer *[animal]
diarrhoea
diarria   diarrhoea
diary *[book]   dairy *[milk]
dibate   debate

Check out di as well

dice
diceive   deceive
dicree   decree
dicshunry   dictionary
dictate   dictation
   [dictating dictated]
dictator   dictatorship
dictionary   dictionaries
did *[do]   died *[die]
dide   died
dident   didn't
didn't [did not]
diduct   deduct

58

die *[death]   dye *[colour]
  [dies dying died]

died *[death]   did *[do]
                    dyed *[colour]

diesel

diet [dieting dieted]

difend   defend

differ [differing differed]

different   differently

difficult

difficulty   difficulties

difrens   difference

difrent   different

dify   defy

dig [digging dug]

digest [digesting digested]

digestion   digestive

digit   digital   digitally

dignify   dignified

dignity

digraph

digree   degree

diing   dyeing *[colour]
                    dying *[about to
                                die]

dijestshun   digestion

dijital   digital

dikshunrey   dictionary

diktater   dictator

dilapidated

dilay   delay

dilect   dialect

dilemma

dilete   delete

diling   dialling

dilinquent   delinquent

dilishus   delicious

dilute [diluting diluted]

dimand   demand

dimensha   dementia

dimension

dimentid   demented

diminish [diminishing diminished]

dimple [dimpled]

din

dinasty   dynasty

dinatime   dinner time

dine [dining dined]

dinghy *[boat]   dingy *[dull]

dingo   dingoes

dingy *[dull]   dinghy *[boat]

dinial   denial

dinner

dinosaur

diodorant   deodorant

dioxide

dip [dipping dipped]

dipacher   departure

dipart   depart

diploma

diplomacy

diplomat   diplomatic

diposzit   deposit

dire

direct [directing directed]

direction   directly

directness   director

directory   directories

dirt   dirty   dirtier

disability   disabilities

disable   disabled

disadvantage

disagree   disagreeable

disagreed   disagreement

disappear   disappearance
   [disappearing disappeared]

disappoint   disappointment
   [disappointing disappointed]

disapproval

disapprove
   [disapproving disapproved]

disarm [disarming disarmed]

disaster   disastrous

disastrously

disbelief

disc *[circle,   disk *[computer]
   music]

discend   descend

discharge [discharging discharged]

disciple

discipline   disciplined

disco   discotheque

discomfort

disconnect [disconnected]

discontented

discotech   discotheque

discount [discounted]

discourage   discouragement
   [discouraging discouraged]

discover   discovery
   [discovering discovered]

discreet   discreetly

discribe · describe

discriminate   discrimination
   [discriminating discriminated]

discripshun   description

discurige   discourage

discus *[throw]

discuss *[talk]   discussion
   [discussing discussed]

disease   diseased

disect   dissect

disembark
  [disembarking disembarked]
disepshun   deception
diseptiv   deceptive
disert   desert *[leave]
                   dessert *[food]
diserve   deserve
diseve   deceive
disgrace [disgracing disgraced]
disgraceful   disgracefully
disgruntled
disguise [disguised]
disgust [disgusting disgusted]
dish   dishes
dishevelled
dishonest   dishonestly
dishonesty
diside   decide
disiduus   deciduous
disillusion [disillusioned]
disine   design
disinfect   disinfectant
  [disinfecting disinfected]
disintegrate   disintegration
  [disintegrating disintegrated]
disirabul   desirable
disire   desire
disjointed

disk *[computer]   disc *[circle,
                            music]
diskomfort   discomfort
dislexsia   dyslexia
dislike [disliked]
dislodge [dislodged]
disloyal
dismal   dismally
dismiss   dismissal
  [dismissing dismissed]
disobedience   disobedient
disobey [disobeying disobeyed]
disorder   disorderly
disorganise [disorganised]
disorganisation
disorientated
disown [disowning disowned]
dispair   despair
dispatch   dispatches
  [dispatching dispatched]
disperse [dispersed]
dispise   despise
dispite   despite
display [displaying displayed]
displeased
dispose   [disposing disposed]
disposable   disposal
dispraxia   dyspraxia

disprove *[deny] disapprove

*[bad]

dispute [disputing disputed]

disqualification

disqualify disqualifies

[disqualifying disqualified]

disregard [disregarded]

disrespectful disrespectfully

disrupt disruption

[disrupting disrupted]

disruptive disruptively

dissapear disappear

dissapoint disappoint

disscurrage discourage

dissect dissection

[dissecting dissected]

dissendent descendant

dissert desert *[leave]

dessert *[food]

dissiplin discipline

dissolve [dissolving dissolved]

dissproov disprove

distance

distant distantly

distilled distillery

distinct distinctly

distinction

distinctive distinctively

distinguish [distinguishes]

[distinguishing distinguished]

distort distortion

[distorting distorted]

distract distraction

[distracting distracted]

distress [distresses]

[distressing distressed]

distribute [distributing distributed]

distribution distributor

district

distroy destroy

distructiv destructive

distrust distrustful

[distrusting distrusted]

disturb disturbance

[disturbing disturbed]

disused

disyfer decipher

ditch ditches [ditching ditched]

ditectiv detective

ditenshun detention

diter deter

ditermin determine

ditest detest

dither [dithering dithered]

dive [diving dived]

divelop develop

diversion

divert [diverting diverted]

divice   device

divide [dividing divided]

divine divinely

divisible

division divisor

divorce [divorcing divorced]

divurtid   diverted

dizease   disease

dizzy dizzier dizziest

dlishus   delicious

do *[act]   doe *[deer]

do [does doing did]

dock [docking docked]

doctor

document documentary
  [documenting documented]

doddery

dodge [dodging dodged]

dodgy dodgier

dodgem

doe *[deer]   dough *[bread]

does doesn't [does not]

dog dogged doggy

doj   dodge

dojem   dodgem

dokter   doctor

dole [doling doled]

dolfin   dolphin

doll dolly dollies

dollar

dollop

dolphin

dome *[shape]   doom *[gloom]

Domesday Book

domestic

dominance dominant

dominate domination
  [dominating dominated]

domino dominoes

donate donation
  [donating donated]

done

donkey donkeys

donor

don't [do not]

doodle [doodling doodled]

doom [doomed]

Doomsday   Domesday *[Book]

door doorknob

dooy   do

dope dopey

dordul   dawdle

dormitory dormitories

dormouse dormice

dorn   dawn

dorter   daughter

dosage

dose *[medicine]   does *[do]

            doze *[nap]

dotty   dottier

double [doubling doubled]

doubly

doubt [doubting doubted]

doubtful   doubtless

dough *[bread]   doe *[deer]

dove   dovecote

dow   do

dowdy   dowdier

down [downing downed]

downstairs   downstream

downwards   downwind

downy

dowtful   doubtful

doze   dozy   dozier

   [dozing dozed]

dozen

drag [dragging dragged]

draggen   dragon

dragon   dragonfly

drain [draining drained]

drainage   drainpipe

drake

drama   dramatic

dramatically

dramatise

  [dramatising dramatised]

drank

drastic   drastically

draught   draughty

draw *[pull, art]

  [drawing drew]

drawer *[box]

drawn   drawn-out

dread [dreading dreaded]

dreadful   dreadfully

dream [dreaming dreamt]

dreamy   dreamier

dreary   drearier

dred   dread

dredge [dredging dredged]

dreem   dream

dregs

drej   dredge

dreme   dream

drench [drenching drenched]

dresarje   dressage

dress [dressing dressed]

dress   dresses   dressmaker

dressage

drew

drey

dribble [dribbling dribbled]

dribiling   dribbling

dride   dried

drie   dry

dried

drier *[less wet]   dryer *[machine]

drift [drifting drifted]

drill [drilling drilled]

drink [drinking drank drunk]

drip [dripping dripped]

drive [driving drove driven]

drizzle [drizzling drizzled]

drone [droning droned]

drool [drooling drooled]

droop *[down]   droopy
 [drooping drooped]

drop *[let fall]

drore   draw *[pull, art]
                        drawer *[box]

drought

drove

drown [drowning drowned]

drowsy   drowsier

drowt   drought

drudge   drudgery

drue   drew

drug [drugging drugged]

drule   drool

drum [drumming drummed]

drunk   drunkenly

dry [dries drying dried]

dryer *[machine]   drier *[less wet]

dryve   drive

du   dew *[drops]
                        do *[get done]
                        due *[owing]

dual *[two]   duel *[fight]
              jewel *[gem]

dub [dubbing dubbed]

dubbul   double

duchess   duchesses

duck [ducking ducked]

duckling

dud

due *[owed]   dew *[drops]
              do *[get done]
              Jew *[religion]

duel *[fight]   dual *[two]

duet

duffel coat

duke

dull   duller   dullness

dum   dumb

dumb   dumber   dumbest

dummy   dummies

65

dump [dumping dumped]

dumpling

dumpy   dumpier

dune

dung

dungarees

dungeon

dunjon   dungeon

duo

Dupiter   Jupiter

duplicate   duplication
  [duplicating duplicated]

during

durt   dirt

dury   jury

dusk   dusky   duskier

dust [dusting dusted]

dusty   dustier

dutiful   dutifully

duty   duties

duv   dove

duvay   duvet

duvet

duwel   dual *[two]
                            duel *[fight]

duz   does

duzn't   doesn't

duzzen   dozen

dwarf   dwarves

dwell [dwelling dwelled dwelt]

dworf   dwarf

Check out
di as well

dye *[colour]   die *[death]

dyeing *[colour]

dying *[death]

dylute   dilute

dynamic

dynamite

dynamo

dynasty

dynosaur   dinosaur

Dyoon   June

dysabul   disable

dysentery

dyslexia   dyslexic

dyspraxia   dyspraxic

Check out
dis as well

each

eager   eagerly   eagerness

eagle   eaglet

ear   ~ache ~phones ~plugs

ear   ~ring ~shot ~wig

eares   ears

early   earlier   earliest

earn *[money]   urn *[vase]

  [earning earned]

earnings

earth   earthly

earthquake

earthworm

eary   eerie *[scary]

          eyrie *[nest]

east   ~erly ~ern ~wards

Easter

easy   easier   easiest   easily

eat [eating ate eaten]

ebb [ebbing ebbed]

eccentric

ech   each

echo [echoes echoing echoed]

ecksact   exact

Check out **ex** as well

ecksamin   examine

ecksaminashun **examination**

ecksampul   **example**

ecksceed   **exceed**

eckscite   **excite**

eclipse

ecology   ecologist

ecsentric   **eccentric**

eczema

edebul   **edible**

edge [edging edged]

edgy   edgier   edgiest

edible

edition *[copy]   addition *[sum]

edj   **edge**

educashun   **education**

education

eel

eer   **ear**

eerie *[scary]   eyrie *[nest]

eerily   eeriness

eese   **ease**

eest   **east**

Eester   **Easter**

eestern   **eastern**

eesy   **easy**

eet   **eat**

eeves   **eaves**

eezee   **easy**

67

efect	effect *[result]
	affect *[alter]
effect *[result]	affect *[alter]
effective effectively	
effectiveness	
efficiency	
efficient efficiently	
effort	
effortless effortlessly	
efishent	efficient
efishuncy	efficiency
efort	effort
eg	egg
ege	edge
egect	eject
eger	eager
egg [egging egged]	
egg ~cup ~shell	
Egipshuns	Egyptians
egsact	exact

Check out ex as well

egsaggerate	exaggerate
egsample	example
egul	eagle
Egyptians	
egzotic	exotic

Eiffel Tower	
eight *[number]	ate *[food]
eighteen eighteenth	
eighth	
eighty eighties eightieth	
eigt	eight
eigth	eighth
either	
eject [ejecting ejected]	
eji	edgy
ekcentrik	eccentric

Check out ec as well

eko	echo
eksampul	example
eksentric	eccentric
eksma	eczema
ekwivalent	equivalent
elament	element
elastic elasticity	
Elastoplast™	
elavatid	elevated
elbow [elbowing elbowed]	
elder elderly eldest	
elderberry elderberries	
eldur	elder
election	

electric   electrical

electrically

electricity   electrician

electricle   electrical

electrify [electrifies]

  [electrifying electrified]

electrocute [electrocuted]

electrocution

electron

electronic   electronically

eleet   elite

elefant   elephant

elekshun   election

elektrik   electric

elektrisitee   electricity

element

elevate [elevated] elevator

eleven   eleventh

elf elves elfin elfish

eligible

eliminate [eliminating eliminated]

Elisabethun   Elizabethan

eliterashun   alliteration

Elizabethan

elk

elm

eloap   elope

elongated

elope [eloping eloped]

else   ~where

elude [eluding eluded]

elushun   illusion

*[fantasy]

allusion *[hint]

email

emarald   emerald

embalm [embalmed]

embankment

embarass   embarrass

embark [embarking embarked]

embarm   embalm

embarrass   embarrassment

  [embarrassing embarrassed]

embassy   embassies

embers

emblem

embrace [embracing embraced]

embrio   embryo

embroider [embroidered]

embroidery

embroyder   embroider

embryo

emerald

emerge [emerging emerged]

emergency   emergencies

emfasis   emphasis

emigrant *[exits] immigrant
*[arrives]

emigrate *[exit] immigrate
*[arrive]

[emigrating emigrated]

emigration   immigration
*[exit]   *[arrival]

emoshun   emotion

emotion

emotional   emotionally

emperor   empress

empire *[lands]   umpire *[game]

employ [employing employed]

employee   employer

employment

emprer   emperor

empty   emptier   emptiest

emrald   emerald

emtee   empty

emu

emurge   emerge

enabel   enable

enable [enabling enabled]

enamel

encampment

enchant enchantment
[enchanting enchanted]

enchantress

enciclopeedia   encyclopaedia

enclose [enclosing enclosed]

enclosure

encoar   encore

encore

encounter
[encountering encountered]

encourage   encouragement
[encouraging encouraged]

encownter   encounter

encyclopaedia   encyclopaedic

end [ending ended]

endanger
[endangering endangered]

endeavour
[endeavouring endeavoured]

endever   endeavour

endid   ended

endless   endlessly

endurance

endure [enduring endured]

enemy   enemies

energetic   energetically

energy   energies

enerjy   energy

enething   anything

enforce [enforcing enforced]

enforse   enforce

engage [engaging engaged]

engagement

Engerlish   English

engine

engineer   engineering

English

engrave [engraving engraved]

engraver

engrossed

engulf [engulfing engulfed]

enjine   engine

enjineer   engineer

enjoy [enjoying enjoyed]

enjoyable   enjoyably

enjoyment

enjure   endure

enkurage   encourage

enlarge [enlarging enlarged]

enlargement

enlist [enlisting enlisted]

enmie   enemy

enormous   enormously

enough

enquire   enquiry

enrage [enraged]

enrol [enrolling enrolled]

ensime   enzyme

ensure [ensuring ensured]

ensyclopeedia   encyclopaedia

entangle [entangled]

enter [entering entered]

enterprise   enterprising

entertain   entertainment

    [entertaining entertained]

enthoosiasum   enthusiasm

enthusiasm   enthusiast

enthusiastic enthusiastically

entire   entirely

entrance   entrant

entrust [entrusting entrusted]

entry   entries

entur   enter

enturtain   entertain

entyre   entire

enuff   enough

enurjetic   energetic

envee   envy

envelop *[surround]

    [enveloping enveloped]

envelope *[paper]

envie   envy

envious   enviously

enviroment   environment

environment

environmental

environmentally

envlope — envelope

envy [envies envying envied]

envyronment — environment

eny — any

enzyme

epic

epidemic

epilepsy epileptic

episewd — episode

episode

epitaph

epitarf — epitaph

eqewstrian — equestrian

equal equally
  [equalling equalled]

equalise equaliser
  [equalising equalised]

equality equalities

equation

equator equatorial

equestrian

equilateral

equilibrium

equinox

equip equipment
  [equipping equipped]

equivalent equivalence

eqwpment — equipment

erase [erasing erased]

eratic — erratic

erer — error

erly — early

ernest — earnest

erode [eroding eroded]

erosion

errand

erratic erratically

error

erth — earth

erupt [erupting erupted]

eruption

esay — essay

escalator

escape [escaping escaped]

eschuary — estuary

escort [escorting escorted]

esculator — escalator

esenshul — essential

eskape — escape

Eskimo

eskort — escort

especially

espinarj — espionage

espionage

essay

essential essentially

establish establishment
[establishing established]

estate

estchury   estuary

esteem [esteemed]

estern   eastern

estimate estimation
[estimating estimated]

estuary estuaries

esy   easy

eternal eternally

eternity

ethnic

ethur   either

eturnity   eternity

euphemism

euro

European

Eurostar™

euthanasia

evacuate evacuation evacuee
[evacuating evacuated]

evade [evading evaded]

evaluate evaluation
[evaluating evaluated]

evaporate evaporation
[evaporating evaporated]

evasive

even evenly evenness

evenchualy   eventually

evening

event eventful

eventual eventually

ever ~green ~lasting ~more

every ~body ~day ~one

every ~thing ~where

evict [evicting evicted]

eviction

evidence

evident evidently

evikt   evict

evil evilly

evning   evening

evolution

evolve [evolving evolved]

evon   even

evrewere   everywhere

evry   every

evur   ever

ewe *[sheep]   you *[person]

          yew *[tree]

exact exactly exactness

exaggerate exaggeration
[exaggerating exaggerated]

exale   exhale

exam examination

examine [examining examined]

example

exasperate exasperation
  [exasperating exasperated]

excavate excavator
  [excavating excavated]

excavation

exceed [exceeding exceeded]

exceedingly

excel [excelling excelled]

excellence excellent

excepshun exception

except [but] accept [take]

exception

exceptional exceptionally

excercise exercise

excershun excursion

excess excessively

exchange [exchanging exchanged]

excitable excitability

excite *[thrill] exit *[out]

excite excitement

excited *[thrilled] exited *[left]

excitedly

exclaim [exclaiming exclaimed]

exclamation

exclude exclusion
  [excluding excluded]

exclusive exclusively

excrement

excrete excretion
  [excreting excreted]

excursion

excuse [excusing excused]

excusable

excwiset exquisite

execute [executing executed]

execution executioner

executive

exekushun execution

exekute execute

exellent excellent

exempt exemption

exercise [exercising exercised]

exert [exerting exerted]

exertion

exhale [exhaling exhaled]

exhaust exhaustion
  [exhausting exhausted]

exhibit exhibitor
  [exhibiting exhibited]

exhibition

exhorst exhaust

exibishun exhibition

exibit exhibit

exile [exiling exiled]

exist [existing existed]

existence   existent

exit *[out]   excite *[thrill]

exitement   excitement

exklude   exclude

exklusiv   exclusive

exkrement   excrement

exkurshun   excursion

exkuse   excuse

exkwisit   exquisite

exorcise [exorcising exorcised]

exorcist   exorcism

exotic

expand   expansion

 [expanding expanded]

expanse

expect   expectation

 [expecting expected]

expectant   expectantly

expectayshun   expectation

expedishun   expedition

expedition

expel [expelling expelled]

expence   expense

expense   expensive

experense   experience

experience

 [experiencing experienced]

experiment   experimentation

 [experimenting experimented]

experimental experimentally

expert   expertly

expertees   expertise

expertise

expire [expiring expired]

expiry

explain [explaining explained]

explanation   explanatory

exploar   explore

explode [exploding exploded]

exploit   exploitation

 [exploiting exploited]

exploration   exploratory

explore [exploring explored]

exploshun   explosion

explosion   explosive

exployt   exploit

export [exporting exported]

express [expressing expressed]

expression   expressionless

expressive   expressively

expulsion

expurt   expert

exquisite   exquisitely

exseed   exceed

exsel   excel

exsellense   excellence

exsept   except

exsert   exert

exsite   excite

extend [extending extended]

extension

extensive   extensively

extent

extention   extension

exterior

exterminate   exterminator
   [exterminating exterminated]

extermination

external   externally

extinct   extinction

extinguish [extinguishes]
   [extinguishing extinguished]

extra   ~terrestrial

extract [extracting extracted]

extraordinarily

extraordinary

extravagance   extravagant

extravagantly

extream   extreme

extreme   extremely

extrordinary   extraordinary

extrovert

exturminate   exterminate

exturnal   external

exurcise   exercise

exurt   exert

eye   ~brow ~lash

eye   ~lid ~liner

eye   ~sight ~witness

Eyemax   Imax™

eyether   either

eyrie *[nest]   eerie *[scary]

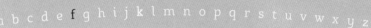

fable

fabric

fabulous

face *[head]

face *[look] [facing faced]

fachen   fashion

fact factual

facter   factor

factor

factory factories

facts *[true]   fax *[paper]

fad

fade [fading faded]

Fahrenheit

faik   fake

fail [failing failed]

failure

faint [fainting fainted]

faintly

fair *[event]   fare *[bus]

fair *[just]

fair fairly fairness

fair-haired

fairground

fairo   Pharoah

fairy *[sprite] fairies

   ferry *[boat]

fairy-godmother

fairytale

faite   fate

faith faithful faithfully

fake [faking faked]

fakt   .   fact

faktoree   factory

falcon falconry

fale   fail

fall [falling fell fallen]

false falsely falseness

famas   famous

fame famed

familiar familiarity

family families

famine

famished

famous famously

fan [fanning fanned]

fanatic

fancy [fancies]

fancy fancier fanciest

fanfare

fang

fansy   fancy

fantasise [fantasising fantasised]

fantastic fantastically

fantasy fantasies

fantisize   fantasise

fantisy   fantasy
fantom   phantom
far *[distant]   fare *[bus]
faraoh   Pharaoh
faraway
farce
fare *[bus]   fair *[event]
farewell
Far East [the]
Farenheight   Fahrenheit
far-fetched
Farisee   Pharisee
farm ~land ~yard
farsen   fasten
farst   fast
fart [farting farted]
farther *[distant] father *[dad]
farthest
fary   fairy
fascinate fascination
  [fascinating fascinated]
fase   face
fashion fashionable
fashionably
fassinate   fascinate
fast [fasting fasted]
fasten [fastening fastened]
fast-forward

fat fatter fattest
fatal fatally
fatality fatalities
fate *[destiny]   fête *[festival]
fateful fatefully
faten   fatten
father *[dad]   farther *[distant]
Father Christmas
fatherhood
father-in-law
fatherly
fatten [fattening fattened]
fatty fattier fattiest
fault faulty faultless
faun *[myths]   fawn *[deer]
fauna
favirite   favourite
favour favourable
favourably
favourite favouritism
favret   favourite
fawlt   fault
fawn *[colour, deer]
fax *[paper]   facts *[true]
  [faxing faxed]
fayr   fair *[just, event]
                fare *[bus]
fayth   faith

faze *[bother]   phase *[stage]
  [fazed]

fead   feed

feal   feel

feald   field

fear [fearing feared]

fearful   fearfully

fearless   fearlessly

feasant   pheasant

feast [feasting feasted]

feat *[action]   feet *[toes]

feather feathered feathery

featherweight

feature [featuring featured]

Febrary   February

February

Febuery   February

fech   fetch

fed

feeblely   feebly

feechure   featur

feed [feeding fed]

feel [feeling felt]

feeld   field

feeler

feend   fiend

feer   fear

feerse   fierce

feest   feast

feet *[toes]   feat *[action]

feetus   foetus

feild   field

feind   fiend

feirce   fierce

fell

fellow

felt   felt-tip

female

femenin   feminine

feminine

feminist   feminism

fence [fencing fenced]

fend [fending fended]

ferm   firm

ferment [fermenting fermented]

fern

fernish   furnish

ferniture   furniture

ferocious   ferociously

feroshus   ferocious

ferret [ferreting ferreted]

Ferris wheel

ferry   ferries

ferst   first

ferther   further

ferthest   furthest

fertile

fertilise   fertilisation
  [fertilising fertilised]

fertility

festival

festive   festivities

fetch [fetching fetched]

fête *[festival]   fate *[destiny]

fether   feather

feud [feuding feuded]

feudal   feudalism

fever

feverish   feverishly

few *[not many]   phew
                   *[exclamation]

fewgitiv   fugitive

fewl   fuel

fewneral   funeral

fewse   fuse

fezant   pheasant

fial   file

fiancé *[man]

fiancée *[lady]

fianl   final

fiansay   fiancé *[man]
          fiancée *[lady]

fiar   fire

fib [fibbing fibbed]

fibre   fibreglass

fibur   fibre

ficks   fix

fickst   fixed

ficshun   fiction

fiction   fictional

fiddle [fiddling fiddled]

fiddly   fiddliest

fidget   fidgety [fidgeting fidgeted]

field [fielding fielded]

field   ~mouse ~work

fiend   fiendish   fiendishly

fier   fear *[afraid]
       fire *[flame]

fierce   fiercer   fiercest

fiercely   fierceness

fierse   fierce

fiery   fierier   fieriest

fif   five

fiftee   fifty

fifteen   fifteenth

fifth

fifty   fifties   fiftieth

fig

figer   figure

figerativ   figurative

figet   fidget

fight [fighting fought]

figurative

figure [figuring figured]

fiksed   fixed

fikshun   fiction

file [filing filed]

fill [filling filled]

fillet

filly   fillies

film [filming filmed]

filosofer   philosopher

filth   filthier   filthiest

filthy

fimail   female

fin *[fish]   Finn *[person]

final *[last]   finally

finale *[last event]

finalist

finarlay   finale

finck   think

find [finding found]

finder

fine [fining fined]

finely

finerly   finally

finger [fingering fingered]

finger   ~nail ~print

finish [finishing finished]

finly   finally

Finn *[person]   fin *[fish]

finsh   finish *[end]

fiord

fir *[tree]   fur *[coat]

fire [firing fired]

fire   ~arm ~brigade

fire extinguisher

fire   ~place ~work

firm firmer firmest

firmly

firn   fern

firry   furry

first   firstly

firsty   thirsty

firther   further

firtile   fertile

firy   fiery

fish [fishing fished]

fisher   fisherman

fishy

fisical   physical

fisics   physics

fist

fit *[clothes]   fight *[hit]

  [fitting fitted]

fit *[strong]   fitness

fite   fight

fiv   five

five

fix [fixes fixing fixed]

fixture

fizz [fizzes fizzing fizzed]

fizzle [fizzling fizzled]

fizzy fizzier fizziest

fjord

flabby flabbier flabbiest

flag [flagging flagged]

flake [flaking flaked]

flame [flaming flamed]

flamingo

flan

flannel

flap [flapping flapped]

flare [flaring flared]

flash [flashes flashing flashed]

flash ~back ~light

flashy flashier flashiest

flask

flat flatter flattest flatly

flatten [flattening flattened]

flatter flattery
  [flattering flattered]

flaunt [flaunting flaunted]

flaver   flavour

flavour [flavouring flavoured]

flaw *[fault]   floor *[base]

flawed flawless

flea *[insect]   flee *[run]

flecks *[dots]   flex *[bend]

flecksibul   flexible

fledgling

flee *[run]   flea *[insect]
  [fleeing fled]

fleece [fleecing fleeced]

fleet

flert   flirt

flesh fleshy

flew *[flight]   flu *[ill]

flewid   fluid

flex *[bend]   flecks *[dots]
  [flexes flexing flexed]

flexible flexibility

flick [flicking flicked]

flicker [flickering flickered]

flick-knife flick-knives

flies

flight *[trip]   flit *[dash]

fliing   flying

flimsy flimsier flimsiest

flinch [flinches flinching flinched]

fling [flinging flung]

flint flinty

flip [flipping flipped]

flippant flippantly

flipper

flirt [flirting flirted]

flisse   fleece

flit *[dash]   flight *[trip]

float [floating floated]

flock [flocking flocked]

floe *[ice]   flow *[river]

flog [flogging flogged]

flood [flooding flooded]

floor *[base]   flaw *[fault]

floot   flute

flop [flopping flopped]

floppy   floppier   floppiest

floral   florist

flornt   flaunt

floss

flote   float

flour *[food]   flower *[bud]

flourish [flourishes]
    [flourishing flourished]

flow *[river]   floe *[ice]
    [flowing flowed]

flower *[plant]   flour *[food]
    [flowering flowered]

flown

flox   flocks

flu *[ill]   flew *[fly]

flud   flood

fluent   fluently

fluff

fluffy   fluffier   fluffiest

fluid

fluke

flume

flung

fluorescent light

flurish   flourish

flush [flushing flushed]

flustered

flute

flutter [fluttering fluttered]

fly *[insect, travel]   flies

fly [flies flying flew flown]

foal

foam [foaming foamed]

fobia   phobia

focus [focuses focusing focused]

fodder

foe

foetus   foetal

fog   foggy

foil [foiling foiled]

foke   folk

foks   fox

fokus   focus

fold [folding folded]

fole   foal

folk ~lore

foll   fall

follow   follower

    [following followed]

fome   foam

fon   phone

fond fonder fondest fondly

fone   phone

fonic   phonic

font

food *[eat]   feud *[fight]

fool [fooling fooled]

foolish   foolishly

foot   ~note ~path ~print

foot   ~step ~wear ~work

football   footballer

for *[use]   fore *[front]

           four *[number]

forbid

   [forbidding forbade forbidden]

forcast   forecast

force [forcing forced]

forceful   forcefully

forchoon   fortune

ford

fore *[front]   for *[use]

           four *[number]

fore   ~arm ~cast ~ground

fore   ~hand ~head ~most

foreboding

foreign   foreigner

foren   foreign

foresee [foresaw foreseen]

forest   forestation

forester   forestry

foretell   foretold

forever

forfeit

forfit   forfeit

forgave

forge [forging forged]

forgery   forgeries

forget [forgetting forgot]

forgetful   forgetfulness

forgive [forgiving forgave forgiven]

forgiveness

forgot   forgotten

forj   forge

fork [forking forked]

forlt   fault

form [forming formed]

formal

formashun   formation

format [formatting formatted]

formation

former formerly	found [founding founded]
formula formulas formulae	foundation
forn	faun *[myths]	fountain

former formerly

formula formulas formulae

forn   faun *[myths]
              fawn *[deer]

forna   fauna

forrest   forest

forse   force

fort *[castle]   fought *[hit]
                thought *[think]

forteen   fourteen

forthcoming

fortnight fortnightly

fortunate fortunately

fortune

forty fortieth

forward forwards

fossil fossilise [fossilised]

foster [fostering fostered]

foto   photo

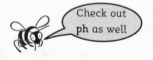
Check out
ph as well

fotograf   photograph

fotosynthesis photosynthesis

fought *[hit]   fort *[castle]
               thought *[think]

foul *[dirty]   fowl *[bird]

fouler foulest

found [founding founded]

foundation

fountain

four *[number]   for *[use]
                fore *[front]

Check out
for as well

fourbid   forbid

fource   force

fourhand   forehand

fourmula   formula

fourt   fought *[hit]
             fort *[castle]
             thought *[think]

fourteen fourteenth

fourth *[4th]   forth *[on]

fourtnight   fortnight

fowl *[bird]   foul *[dirty]

fownd   found

fowntain   fountain

fox foxes

foyl   foil

fraction

fracture [fracturing fractured]

frael   frail

fragile

fragment

fragrance   fragrant

fragrense   fragrance

frail   frailer   frailest

frajile   fragile

fraksher   fracture

frakshun   fraction

frale   frail

frame [framing framed]

frank frankly frankness

frankfurter

frankincense

frantic   frantically

frase   phrase

fraud   fraudster

fraught

freak   freakish

freckle   freckled

free [freeing freed]

freedom

freer   freest   freely

freestyle

freeze *[ice]   frieze *[strip]
   [freezing froze frozen]

freezer

freind   friend

frekwency   frequency

frekwent   frequent

french

french fries

frend   friend

frens   friends

frenzy   frenzied

frequency   frequencies

frequent   frequently

fresh   fresher   freshest

freshen [freshening freshened]

freshly   freshness

fret *[mope]   threat *[warn]
   [fretting fretted]

frew   threw *[ball]

              through *[go
                      through]

friar   friary

frickshun   friction

friction

Friday

fridge

fried

friend ~less ~ship

friendly friendlier friendliest

frieze *[strip]   freeze *[ice]

frigate

frige   fridge

fright *[fear]

frighten [frightening frightened]

frightful   frightfully

frill frilly frilliest

fringe fringed

Frisbee™

frisk [frisking frisked]

frisky friskier friskiest

fritter [frittering frittered]

frivolous

frizzy frizzier frizziest

frog ~man ~spawn

frogmarch [frogmarched]

frolic [frolicked frolicking]

from

frong   throng

front

frontier

froot   fruit

frord   fraud

frorght   fraught

frost [frosting frosted]

frostbite frostbitten

frosty frostier frostiest

froth [frothing frothed]

frothy

frown [frowning frowned]

froze frozen

fruit

fruitful fruitfulness

fruitless fruitlessly

fruity fruitier fruitiest

frunt   front

fruntier   frontier

frustrate frustration
  [frustrating frustrated]

frut   fruit

fry [frying fried]

fryer frying pan

fryt   fright

fucher   future

fud   food

fude   feud

fudge

fue   few

fuel [fuelling fuelled]

fugitive

ful   fool *[idiot]
                 full *[complete]

fule   fuel

fulfil [fulfilling fulfilled]

full *[up]   fool *[idiot]

fullness fully

fumble [fumbling fumbled]

fume [fuming fumed]

fun

function [functioning functioned]

fund [funding funded]

funeral

fungus   fungi

funkshun   function

funnel

funny   funnier   funniest

fur *[coat]   fir *[tree]

furious   furiously

furn   fern

furnace

furnish [furnishes]

  [furnishing furnished]

furniture

furoshus   ferocious

furry *[hairy]   fury *[anger]

furrier   furriest

furst   first

further   furthest

furthering

furthermore

furtile   fertile

furtilise   fertilise

fury *[anger]   furry *[hairy]

fuse [fusing fused]

fuss *[worry]   fuzz *[fluff]

  [fusses fussing fussed]

fussy   fussier   fussiest

fut   foot

future

fuzz

fuzzy   fuzzier   fuzziest

fyfty   fifty

fynd   find

fysical   physical

fysics   physics

fyve   five

Check out
fi as well

gabble [gabbling gabbled]

gadget

gael   gale

gag [gagging gagged]

gage   gauge

gaggle

gaily

gain [gaining gained]

gaip   gape

gajet   gadget

gala

galaxy   galactic

gale   gale-force

galery   gallery

galleon

gallery   galleries

galley

gallon

gallop [galloping galloped]

gallows

galy   gaily *[merrily]
               galley *[ship]

gamble *[games]
   [gambling gambled]

gambol *[frolic]
   [gambolling gambolled]

game

gammon

gander

gang   ~plank ~way

gangly

gangster

gap *[space]   gap-toothed

gape *[look, open] [gaping gaped]

garage

garantey   guarantee

garbage

gard   guard

garden   gardening

gardian   guardian

gargle *[throat] [gargling gargled]

gargoyle *[carving]

garige   garage

garland

garlic   garlicky

garment

garrison

gas

gase   gaze

gash   gashes

gasp [gasping gasped]

gastly   ghastly

gate

gateau   gateaux

gatecrash   gatecrasher

gather [gathering gathered]

89

gattoe   gateau

gaugius   gorgeous

gave

gawky

gayn   gain

gayt   gate

gaze [gazing gazed]

gear   ~box ~stick

geek   geeky

geese

gel

gelignite

gelly   jelly

gem

Gemini

gender

general

generation

generosity

generous   generously

genes *[DNA]   jeans *[denim]

genetic

genetic engineering

genetically modified

genie

genius

genral   general

gent

gentle   gentleness

gentleman

genuine   genuinely

geography

geology   geologist

geometry

geranium

gerbil

gergle   gurgle

geriatric

gerila   gorilla

gerl   girl

germ

German

germinate   germination

   [germinating germinated]

gess   guess

gest   guessed

        *[estimated]

        guest *[visitor]

gesture

get [getting got]

getto   ghetto

gewel   jewel

Check out je as well

gewelry   jewellery

gewish | Jewish

geyser

ghastly ghastliest

ghetto ghetto blaster

ghost ghostly

ghoul ghoulish

giant

gibbering gibberish

gidanse | guidance

giddy giddiness

gide | guide

gier | gear

gift

gig *[show] | jig *[dance]

gigabyte

gigantic

giggle *[ha ha] | jiggle *[jog]

gilotine | guillotine

gilt *[gold] | guilt *[shame]

giltey | guilty

gin

ginee pig | guinea pig

ginger gingerly gingery

gingham

giraffe

girgul | gurgle

girl girlfriend girlie

giro *[bank] | gyro *[spins]

gise | guise

gist *[idea] | jest *[joke]

gitar | guitar

give [giving gave given]

giy | guy

Giy Forks | Guy Fawkes

glacier glacial

glad gladly gladness

gladiator

glaisha | glacier

glamour glamorous

glance [glancing glanced]

gland glandular fever

glare [glaring glared]

glarnse | glance

glars | glass

glass glasses glassful

glazier

gleam [gleaming gleamed]

glide [gliding glided]

glimmer [glimmering]

glimpse [glimpsed]

glimsped | glimpsed

glint

glisten [glistening glistened]

glitter [glittering glittered]

gloat [gloating gloated]

global globally

globe

gloom   gloomy

gloomier   gloomiest

glossy   glossier   glossiest

glove

glow   glow-worm

glucose

glue [gluing glued]

glutton

gnarled

gnat

gnaw *[bite]   nor *[neither]

  [gnawing gnawed]

gnome   gnomish

go [goes going went]

go   go-kart

goal   goalie   goalkeeper

goat

gob   ~smacked ~stopper

gobble [gobbling gobbled]

gobbledegook

goblin

God

god   ~dess ~child ~daughter

god   ~father ~mother ~parent

god   ~send ~son

goggle [goggling goggled]

goggle-eyed

gold   ~fish ~mine

golden

golf   golf course

gon   gone

gone   goner

good goodness

goodbye

Good Friday

gooey

gool   ghoul

goose   goose pimples

gooseberry   gooseberries

gorge [gorging gorged]

gorgeous

gorilla

gory   goriest

gosling

gospel

gossip

gost   ghost

got

goul   ghoul

government

gowing   going

grab [grabbing grabbed]

grace   graceful   gracefully

grade

gradual   gradually

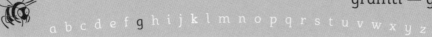
graf   graph
graffiti
graid   grade
grail
grain   grainy
gram
grammar
grammatically
granade   grenade
granchild   grandchild
grand   ~child ~children
grand   ~daughter ~father
grand   ~ma ~mother ~pa
grand   ~parent ~son ~stand
grandad
granny   grannies
graph
grapple [grappling grappled]
gras   grass
grase   grace *[goodness]
                graze *[feed, cut]
grasp [grasping grasped]
grass   grassy   grasshopper
grate *[fire]   great *[big]
grateful   gratefully
grater *[cheese]   greater *[bigger]
gratest   greatest
gratichewd   gratitude

gratitude
grave   gravely
grave   ~digger ~stone ~yard
gravel   gravelly
gravity
gravy
gray   grey
grayn   grain
graze
grdon   garden
grease   ~paint ~proof
greasy
great *[big]   grate *[fire]
greater
greatly   greatness
greed   greedier   greediest
greedy   greedily
green   greenery
green   ~grocer ~house
greenhouse
greese   grease
greet   greetings
greif   grief
greive   grieve
gremlin
gren   green
grenade
grew

grewsome   gruesome

grey   ~hound

grief   grief-stricken

grieve [grieving grieved]

grill [grilling grilled]

grim *[bad]

grime *[dirt]

grimy   grimiest

grin [grinning grinned]

grind [grinding ground]

grip [gripping gripped]

grit   gritty

grizzly

groan *[moan]   grown *[up]
   [groaning groaned]

grocer   groceries   grocery

groggy   groggier

grone   groan *[moan]
            grown *[up]

groom

groop   group

groosum   gruesome

groove *[slot]   grove *[trees]

grope [groping groped]

groser   grocer

gross   grossly

grotto   grottos

grotty   grottier   grottiest

ground   ~less ~sheet ~sman

group

grouse

grove *[wood]   groove *[slot]

grovel [grovelling grovelled]

grow   growing

growl [growling growled]

grown *[up]   groan *[moan]

grownd   ground

growth

grub

grubby   grubbier   grubbiest

grudge   grudgingly

grue   grew

gruesome

gruff   gruffly

gruge   grudge

grumble [grumbling grumbled]

grumpy   grumpier
   grumpiest

grunt [grunting grunted]

grupe   group

guarantee   guarantees
   [guaranteeing guaranteed]

guard   guardsman

guardian

gud   good

guess [guessing guessed]

guessed *[estimated]*

guest *[visitor]*

guidance

guide ~book ~lines
  [guiding guided]

guillotine

guilt *[shame]*   gilt *[gold]*

guilty guiltier guiltiest

guinea pig

guitar guitarist

gulf Gulf stream

gull

gully gullies

gulp [gulping gulped]

gum ~shield

gun ~boat ~dog ~fight ~fire

gun ~man ~point ~powder

gun ~ship ~shot

gurbil   gerbil

gurgle [gurgling gurgled]

gurl   girl

guseberry   gooseberry

gush [gushes gushing gushed]

gust gusty

gutter guttering

guvern   govern

guverment   government

guy Guy Fawkes

guzzle [guzzling guzzled]

gym gymnasium

gymkhana

gymnast gymnastics

gypsy gypsies

H-bomb

habit

habitat   habitation

hack [hacking hacked]

hackles

hacksaw

had   hadn't [had not]

haev   have

haf   have

hag   haggard

haggis

haggle [haggling haggled]

hail [hailing hailed]

hailstone

hair *[head]   hare *[animal]

hair   ~brush ~cut ~dresser

hairy   hairier   hairiest

half   halves

half   ~hour ~way

hall *[room]   haul *[pull]

hall   ~mark ~way

Halloween

hallucinate   hallucination
   [hallucinating hallucinated]

halo   haloes

halt [halting halted]

halve [halving halved]

ham   ~burger

hammer [hammering hammered]

hammock

hamster

hand [handing handed]

hand   ~bag ~book ~ful

hand   ~made ~shake ~stand

handcuff [handcuffed]

handicap [handicapped]

handkerchief   hanky

handle [handling handled]

handsome   handsomest

handwriting   handwritten

handy   handier   handiest

handyman

hang [hanging hung]

hangar *[plane]

hanger *[clothes]

hankercheif   handkerchief

hankuff   handcuff

hanriting   handwriting

hanshake   handshake

hansome   handsome

hapand   happened

haphazard   haphazardly

hapon   happen

hapond   happened

happen [happening happened]

happy   happier   happiest

harbour

hard   harder   hardest

hard   ~board ~ship

harden [hardening hardened]

hardly   hardness

hardy   hardier   hardiest

hare *[animal]   hair *[head]

harf   half

harm [harming harmed]

harmful   harmfully

harmless   harmlessly

harmony   harmonies

harness   harnesses
  [harnessing harnessed]

harp   harpist

harpoon [harpooned]

harrier jet

harsh   harsher   harshest

harshly   harshness

hartless   heartless

harvest [harvesting harvested]

has   hasn't [has not]

hassle [hassling hassled]

haste

hasty   hastier   hastiest

hat *[head]   hate *[dislike]

hatch [hatches hatching hatched]

hatchet

hate *[dislike]   hat *[head]
  [hating hated]

hateful

hath   have

hatred

haul *[pull]   hall *[room]
  [hauling hauled]

haunches

haunt [haunting haunted]

have [has having had]

haven

haven't [have not]

havoc

hawk

hawse   hoarse *[voice]
          horse *[animal]

hay *[grass]   hey *[greet]

hay   ~stack ~wire

hayl   hail *[ice]

hazard

haze hazy hazier hazily

hazel

he   he's [he is, has]

head [heading headed]

headache

head   ~dress ~light ~line

head   ~master ~mistress

head   ~phones ~quarters

heal *[cure]   heel *[foot]
[healing healed]
healer
health healthy healthily
healthier healthiest
heap [heaping heaped]
hear *[sound]   here *[place]
[hearing heard]
heard *[ear]   herd *[animals]
hearse
heart ~beat ~breaking
heart ~broken
heartily
heartless heartlessly
hearty heartier heartiest
heat [heating heated] heater
heather
heave [heaving heaved]
heaven heavenly
heavily heaviness
heavy heavier heaviest
Hebrew
hectare
hectic
he'd [he had, would]
hed   head
hedge [hedging hedged]
hedge ~hog ~row

heds   heads
heel *[foot]   he'll *[he will]
heer   hear
heffer   heifer
hefty heftier heftiest
heifer
height
heighten [heightened]
heir *[inherits]   hair *[head]
heiress heirloom
heksagon   hexagon
held
helicopter helipad heliport
helium
he'll [he will, shall]
hell *[devil]   heel *[foot]
hello *[greet]   halo *[light]
helm helmsman
helmet
help [helping helped]
helper helpful helpfully
helpfulness
helpless helplessly
helplessness
helter-skelter
helth   health
hemisphere
hen ~pecked

her *[female]   here *[place]

herald [heralding heralded]

herb   herbal

herbivore   herbivorous

herd *[animals]   heard *[ear]
  [herding herded]

herdul   hurdle

here *[place]   hear *[sound]

herl   hurl

hermit   hermitage

hero   heroes

heroic   heroically

heroine

heroism

heron

herry   hairy

hers *[she owns]

herself

hert   hurt

hertul   hurtle

hesitant   hesitantly

hesitate   hesitation
  [hesitating hesitated]

heven   heaven

hevy   heavy

hexagon   hexagonal

hey *[greet]   hay *[grass]

hi *[greet]   high *[tall]

hibernate   hibernation
  [hibernating hibernated]

hiccup [hiccupping hicupped]

hid *[past of hide]

hide *[not seen]   [hiding]
  [hid, hidden]

hideous   hideously

hidrolik   hydraulic

hieght   height

hiena   hyena

hier   hear *[sound]
                   here *[place]
                   higher *[taller]
                   hire *[employ]

hieroglyphics

hiest   highest

higeen   hygiene

higgledy-piggledy

high *[tall]   hi *[greet]

high   ~chair ~lands ~lighter

higher *[taller]   hire *[employ]

highest   highly

highlight [highlighting highlighted]

Highness

hights   heights

highway   ~man ~men

hijack   hijacker
  [highjacking highjacked]

hike [hiking hiked]

hilarious

hill ~side

hilly hillier hilliest

hilt

him *[male]   hymn *[song]

himself

hind ~quarters ~sight

hinder [hindering hindered]

Hindu Hinduism

hinge [hinging hinged]

hint [hinting hinted]

hip

hiper   hyper

hippopotamus

hir   her *[female]
       hire *[employ]

hirdel   hurdle

hire *[employ]   higher *[taller]
  [hiring hired]

hirl   hurl

his *[he owns]

hiss *[sound] hisses
  [hissing hissed]

histeria   hysteria

histerical   hysterical

historian

historic historical

history histories

hit [hitting hit] hitter

hitch [hitches hitching hitched]

hitch-hike hitch-hiker
  [hitch-hiking hitch-hiked]

hite   height

hiten   heighten

hive

hiway   highway

hiy   high

ho *[shout]   hoe *[dig]

hoaks   hoax

hoal   whole

hoard *[store]   horde *[mass]
  [hoarding hoarded]

hoarse *[voice]   horse *[ride]

hoarsely hoarseness

hoax hoaxes
  [hoaxing hoaxed]

hobble [hobbling hobbled]

hobby hobbies

hockey

hoe *[dig]   ho *[shout]
  [hoeing hoed]

hog [hogging hogged]

Hogmanay

hoist [hoisting hoisted]

hokey   hockey

hold [holding held]   holder

hole *[gap]   whole *[full]

holey *[holes]   holy *[sacred]
                     wholly *[fully]

holiday

holier   holiest

hollow [hollowing hollowed]

holly *[tree]   holy *[sacred]
                     wholly *[fully]

Hollywood

holocaust

hologram

holster

holy *[sacred]   holly *[tree]
                     wholly *[fully]

homage

home   homely

homeless   homelessness

home-made

homesick   homesickness

homework

homige   homage

homonym

homophone

honer   honour

honest   honestly   honesty

honey   ~comb ~moon ~suckle

honk [honking honked]

honour [honouring honoured]

honourable   honourably

hood   hooded

hoof   hooves

hook [hooking hooked]

hooligan   hooliganism

hoop *[circle]   whoop *[shout]

hoot [hooting hooted]

hooter

hoover™ [hoovering hoovered]

hop *[jump]   hope *[wish]
  [hopping hopped]

hope [hoping hoped]

hopeful   hopefully

hopeless   hopelessly

hopital   hospital

hopskotch

horde *[mass]   hoard *[store]

horer   horror

horibul   horrible

horid   horrid

horific   horrific

horizon

horizontal   horizontally

hork   hawk

horl   hall *[room]
                     haul *[pull]

hormone

101

horn   horned

hornches   haunches

hornet

hornt   haunt

horor   horror

horoscope

horrible   horribly

horrid   horridly

horrific   horrifically

horrify [horrifies]

  [horrifying horrified]

horror

horse *[animal]   hoarse *[voice]

horse   ~fly ~hair ~power

horse   ~shoe ~whip

horthorn   hawthorn

hose *[water]   hoes *[digs]

hosed

hospital

host [hosting hosted]

hostage

hostel

hostess   hostesses

hostile

hostility   hostilities

hot   hotter   hottest   hotly

hotel

hot-tempered

houes   house

hound [hounding hounded]

hour *[time]   our *[owns]

hourly

hours *[time]   ours *[owns]

hourse   hours

house [housing housed]

house   ~ful ~hold ~keeper

house   ~plant ~proud

house-trained

housewife   housework

House of Commons

House of Lords

hovel

hover [hovering hovered]

how *[how much]   who *[?]

however

howl [howling howled]

hownd   hound

howse   house

hoyst   hoist

hu   who *[?]

huch   hutch

hud   hood

huddle [huddling huddled]

huff

hug *[clasp]   huge *[large]

  [hugging hugged]

hugely hugeness

huj   huge

huligan   hooligan

hulk hulking

hull

hum [humming hummed]

human *[person]

humane *[caring] humanely

humble humbly

humbug

humer   humour

humid humidity

humiliate humiliation
  [humiliating humiliated]

humility

humorous

humour [humouring humoured]

hump ~back

hunch hunches
  [hunching hunched]

hundred hundredth

huney   honey

hung

hunger hungrier hungriest

hungry hungrily

hunk

hunny   honey

hunt [hunting hunted]

hunter

huntsman

hurbivor   herbivore

Check out
her as well

hurd   heard *[sound]
                       herd *[animals]

hurdle [hurdling hurdled]

huriball   horrible

hurikane   hurricane

hurl [hurling hurled]

hurmit   hermit

hurray

hurricane

hurry hurriedly
  [hurries hurrying hurried]

hurse   hearse

hurt [hurting hurt]

hurtful

hurtle [hurtling hurtled]

husband

hush [hushed]

husk

husky huskier huskiest

hussel   hustle

hustle [hustling hustled]

hut

hutch	hutches	hymn *[song]	him *[male]
huver	hoover™	hynd	hind
hy	hi	hyper	~active ~market
hybernate	hibernate	hyphen	

Check out
hi as well

		hypnosis	hypnotic
		hypnotise [hypnotising hypnotised]	
		hypnotist	hypnotism
hyde	hide	hypochondria	hypochondriac
hydraulic		hypocrisy	hypocrite
hydrogen		hypotenuse	
hyena		hypothermia	
hyer	higher *[taller]	hyre	higher *[taller]
	hire *[employ]		hire *[employ]
hyest	highest	hysteria	hysterics
hygiene	hygienist	hysterical	hysterically
hygienic		hyt	height
hyjack	hijack	hyway	highway
hyke	hike		

104

I *[me]   eye *[see]
ice *[cold]   eyes *[see]
  [icing iced]
iceberg
icee   icy
ich   itch
icicle
iclispe   eclipse
iconomy   economy
icy icier iciest
icycul   icicle
I'd [I had, would]
idea
ideal ideally
idear   idea
identical identically
identify [identified]
identity identities
idiot idiotic
idle *[lazy]   idol *[worship]
idly
idolise [idolising idolised]
idyllic
idyot   idiot
iether   either *[or]
if
igloo
ignerence   ignorance

ignition
ignor   ignore
ignorance ignorant
ignore [ignoring ignored]
ignorens   ignorance
ignorent   ignorant
iject   eject
iland   island
ilastic   elastic
ile   aisle *[passage]
                isle *[island]
I'le   I'll *[I will, shall]
ilegal   illegal
ilegibul   illegible
I'll *[I will, shall] isle *[island]
                aisle *[walk]
ill iller illest
illegal illegally
illegible illegibly
illness
illuminations
illustrate illustrator
    [illustrating illustrated]
illustration
ilope   elope
ilustrashun   illustration
I'm [I am]
imaculate   immaculate

image   imagery
imaginary [imagining imagined]
imagination   imaginative
imagine   imaginable
imature   immature
imedeate   immediate
imens   immense
imerse   immerse
imige   image
imigrate   immigrate
imitate imitation imitator
  [imitating imitated]
immaculate   immaculately
immature   immaturity
immediate   immediately
immense   immensely
immigrant *[in] emigrant *[out]
immigrate *[in] emigrate *[out]
immigration   emigration
          *[in]   *[out]
immobile
immoral
immortal   immortality
immoshun   emotion
immune   immunity
immunise [immunised]
imorul   immoral
imp   impish

impact
impale [impaled]
impashens   impatience
impatience
impatient   impatiently
impechuous   impetuous
impede [impeding impeded]
imperfect   imperfectly
impersonate
  [impersonating impersonated]
impersonation   impersonator
impertinence   impertinent
impervious
impetuous   impetuously
implament   implement
implication
implore [imploring implored]
imply   implication
  [implying implied]
impolite   impoliteness
import [importing imported]
importance
important   importantly
impose [imposing imposed]
impossible   impossibly
impossibul   impossible
impostor
impourtant   important

impractical

impresiv   impressive

impress [impressing impressed]

impression   impressionable

impressionism   impressionist

impressive   impressively

imprison [imprisoned]

imprisonment

improbable

improper   improperly

impropur   improper

improve [improving improved]

improvement

improvise   improvisation
   [improvising improvised]

impruve   improve

impulse

impulsive   impulsively

impulsiveness

impure

impursonate   impersonate

impurtinents   impertinence

imunise   immunise

in *[go in]   inn *[pub]

inability

inaccessible

inaccurate   inaccurately

inacsessibul   inaccessible

inactive   inactivity

inacurate   inaccurate

inadequate   inadequately

inaksessible   inaccessible

inaktivity   inactivity

inappropriate   inappropriately

inattentive

inbarits   embarrassed

in-between

incapable

incense [incensed]

incensitiv   insensitive

incentive

incequre   insecure

incesant   incessant

incessant   incessantly

inch   inches

inchuitiv   intuitive

incident   incidentally

incignificant   insignificant

incincere   insincere

incision

incist   insist

incline   inclination
   [inclining inclined]

include   inclusion
   [including included]

incoherent

income incoming

incompatible

incompetence

incompetent incompetently

incomplete incompletely

inconceivable inconceivably

inconcistent inconsistent

inconclusive

inconsiderate

inconsiderit inconsiderate

inconsistency inconsistencies

inconsistent inconsistently

inconsolable

inconspicuous

inconspicuously

inconvenient

incorrect incorrectly

increase increasingly

  [increasing increased]

incredible incredibly

incubate incubator

  [incubating incubated]

incubation

incurable incurably

indecent indecently

indecisive

indeed

indefinite indefinitely

indeks index

independence

independent independently

inderstre industry

indescribable indescribably

indesent indecent

indesisiv indecisive

indestructible

index indices [indexing indexed]

Indian

indicate indication

  [indicating indicated]

indicator

indicision indecision

indigestion indigestible

indignant

indigo

indijestion indigestion

indikate indicate

indikayshun indication

indirect indirectly

indiscreet indiscretion

indiscribabul indescribable

indisputable

indistinct indistinctly

indistructabul indestructible

individual individually

individuality

indoor indoors
indulge indulgence
 [indulging indulged]
indulgent
industree industry
industrial
industrious industriously
industry industries
indyrect indirect
ineckspensiv inexpensive
inecksperiens inexperience
inedible
inefectiv ineffective
ineffective ineffectively
inefficiency
inefficient inefficiently
inekscusabul inexcusable
inekspensiv inexpensive
ineksperience inexperience
inept ineptly
inequality inequalities
iner inner
inescapable inescapably
inevitability
inevitable inevitably
inexcusable
inexpensive inexpensively
inexperience inexperienced

inexplicable inexplicably
infachuated infatuated
infamous infamously
infancy
infant infantile
infantry
infatuated infatuation
infect [infecting infected]
infection
infectious infectiously
infekshus infectious
infekt infect
infent infant
infentry infantry
infer [inferring inferred]
inference
inferior inferiority
inferno
infertile infertility
infest [infested]
infidel
infidelity infidelities
infinite infinitely
infinitee infinity
infinitive
infinity
infirier inferior
infirno inferno

inflamabul   inflammable

inflame inflammable
 [inflaming inflamed]

inflammation

inflashun   inflation

inflate inflatable
 [inflating inflated]

inflation

inflaym   inflame

inflayt   inflate

inflewnce   influence

inflexible

inflict [inflicting inflicted]

influence [influencing influenced]

influenshall   influential

influential

inform informative
 [informing informed]

informal informality

informally

informant

informashun   information

information

infrared

infrequent infrequently

infuriate [infuriating infuriated]

ingenious ingeniously

ingenuity

ingrained

ingratitude

ingredient

ingreedyent   ingredient

ingury   injury

inhabit inhabitant
 [inhabiting inhabited]

inhail   inhale

inhalation

inhale [inhaling inhaled]

inherit [inherited]

inheritance

inhibit inhibition
 [inhibiting inhibited]

inhospitable

inings   innings

inishiate   initiate

inishul   initial

initial initially

initiate initiation
 [initiating initiated]

initiative

inject injection
 [injecting injected]

injenious   ingenious

injer   injure

injery   injury

injure [injuring injured]

injury injuries

injustice

ink inky

inkling

inklude   include

Check out
inc as well

inkrease   increase

inkredibul   incredible

inkurabul   incurable

inkwest   inquest

inland

in-laws

inlay inlaid

inlet

inlore   in-law

inmate

inn *[pub]   in *[go in]

innability   inability

innaccurate   inaccurate

innedibul   inedible

inner innermost

innevitabul   inevitable

innings

innocence

innocent innocently

innoculate   inoculate

innosent   innocent

innovation

innumerable

innundate   inundate

inocent   innocent

inoculate inoculation
  [inoculating inoculated]

inoffensive

inokulate   inoculate

inormity   enormity

inormous   enormous

input [inputting input]

inquest

inquire inquiry

inquisitive inquisitively

inquisitiveness

insane insanely

insanity

inscription

insect

insecure insecurely

insecurity insecurities

insekt   insect

insekure   insecure

insensitive insensitively

insensitivity

insentiv   incentive

inseparable

111

insert   insertion
  [inserting inserted]
insessant   incessant
inside
insidens   incidents
insident   incident
insight   incite *[stir up]
  *[understanding]
insignificance
insignificant   insignificantly
insincere   insincerely
insincerity
insipid   insipidness
insishun   incision
insist insistent [insisting insisted]
insistence   insistently
insite   incite *[stir up]
                  insight
                  *[understanding]
insolant   insolent
insolence
insolent   insolently
insomnia   insomniac
insomya   insomnia
inspect inspection inspector
  [inspecting inspected]
inspekt   inspect
inspektor   inspector

inspire   inspiration
  [inspiring inspired]
install [installing installed]
instalment
instance   instants
  *[example]   *[moments]
instant   instantly
instead
instinct
institushun   institution
institute
institution   institutional
instorl   install
instrement   instrument
instruct [instructing instructed]
instruction   instructor
instrukt   instruct
instrument   instrumental
insufficient   insufficiently
insufishent   insufficient
insulate   insulation
  [insulating insulated]
insulayt   insulate
insulin
insult [insulting insulted]
insurance
insure *[cover]   ensure *[be sure]
  [insuring insured]

insurt   insert

intact

intake

intakt   intact

inteereer   interior

integrait   integrate

integrate   integration

   [integrating integrated]

integrity

intelecchual   intellectual

inteligense   intelligence

inteligent   intelligent

intellectual   intellectually

intelligence

intelligent   intelligently

intend [intending intended]

intense   intensely

intenshun   intention

intenshunal   intentional

intensity

intensive   intensively

intention   intentional

intentionally

interact   interaction

   [interacting interacted]

interactive

interagayshun   interrogation

interest [interesting interested]

interface

interfere   interference

   [interfering interfered]

interior

interminable   interminably

intermission

intermittent   intermittently

internal   internally

internashunal   international

international   internationally

Internet

interogate   interrogate

interpret   interpretation

   [interpreting interpreted]

interrogate [interrogated]

interrogation

interrupt   interruption

   [interrupting interrupted]

intersect   intersection

   [intersecting intersected]

intersperse [interspersed]

interval

intervene   intervention

   [intervening intervened]

interview

   [interviewing interviewed]

intervue   interview

interweave [interwoven]

intestine

intimait   intimate

intimate   intimately

intimidate   intimidation

   [intimidating intimidated]

intirier   interior

into

intolerable   intolerably

intolerance   intolerant

intolrabul   intolerable

intolrance   intolerance

intoxicated   intoxication

intreeg   intrigue

intrepid   intrepidly

intrest   interest

intricate   intricately

intrigue [intriguing intrigued]

intrikit   intricate

introduce

  [introducing introduced]

introduction   introductory

introjuce   introduce

introod   intrude

introoshun   intrusion

introvert   introverted

intrude [intruding intruded]

intrushun   intrusion

intrusion   intrusive

intuishun   intuition

intuition

inturest   interest

Check out **inter** as well

inturfeer   interfere

inturmishun   intermission

inturnal   internal

Inturnet   Internet

inturpret   interpret

inturvue   interview

intwinded   entwined

Inuit

inumerabul   innumerable

invade [invading invaded]

invalid

invaluable

invashun   invasion

invasion

invayd   invade

invent   invention   inventor

  [inventing invented]

inventive   inventiveness

invertebrate

invert [inverted]

invest investment investor

  [investing invested]

investigate   investigation
 [investigating investigated]
investigator
invirtibrate   invertebrate
invisibility
invisible   invisibly
invite   invitation
 [inviting invited]
involuntary   involuntarily
involuntry   involuntary
involve [involving involved]
involvement
invurtebrate   invertebrate
inward   inwardly   inwards
inwud   inward
iradicate   eradicate
irase   erase
irate   irately
irational   irrational

Check out
irr as well

iregular   irregular
irelevent   irrelevant
ireplaceabul   irreplaceable
iresistibul   irresistible
iresponsibul   irresponsible
ireversibul   irreversible

irigate   irrigate
Irish
iritabul   irritable
iritate   irritate
irly   early
irn   earn *[money]
                 urn *[vase]
irnest   earnest
irning   ironing
iron [ironing ironed]
ironic   ironically
ironik   ironic
ironmongers
irony
irrashunal   irrational
irrate   irate
irrational   irrationally
irregular   irregularly
irregularity   irregularities
irrelevant   irrelevance
irresistible   irresistibly
irresponsible   irresponsibly
irreverent   irreverently
irreversible
irrigate   irrigation
 [irrigating irrigated]
irritability
irritable   irritably

irritate   irritation
  [irritating irritated]

irth   earth

ise   ice *[cold]
                eyes *[see]

ishue   issue

isicul   icicle

ising   icing

Islam   Islamic

island   islander

isle *[island]   aisle *[passage]

isn't [is not]

isolashun   isolation

isolate [isolating isolated]

isolation

isosceles triangle

isosulees   isosceles

issue [issuing issued]

isue   issue

it

italics

itch [itching itched]

itchy

item

iternal   eternal

iternity   eternity

ither   either

it'll [it will, shall]

its *[belongs]   it's *[it is, has]

itself

iturnity   eternity

ivacuate   evacuate

ivaluate   evaluate

ivaporate   evaporate

I've [I have]

ivolve   evolve

ivory

ivry   ivory

ivy

iye   I *[me]
                  eye *[see]

iznt   isn't [is not]

jab [jabbing jabbed]

jack ~daw ~knife ~pot

jackal

jacket

jagged

jaguar

jail [jailing jailed] jailer

jak   jack

jaket   jacket

jale   jail

jam [jamming jammed]

Janery   January

jangle [jangling jangled]

January

Janyorary   January

jar [jarring jarred]

jargon

javelin

jaw jawbone

jazz jazzy

jealous jealously jealousy

Check out ge as well

jeans *[denim]   genes *[DNA]

jeer [jeering jeered]

jelisy   jealousy

jelly jellies jellied

jellyfish

jelus   jealous

jentil   gentle

jeriatric   geriatric

jerk [jerking jerked]

jerky jerkier jerkiest

jernal   journal

jerney   journey

jersey

jest [jesting jested] jester

Jesus Christ

jet [jetting jetted]

jet-propelled

jetty jetties

Jew *[religion]   dew *[drops]
                   due *[owing]

jewel *[gem]   dual *[two]
                   duel *[fight]

jewelled

jeweller jewellery

Jewish

jewn   June

jier   jeer

jig [jigging jigged]

jiggle [jiggling jiggled]

jigsaw

jilt [jilted]

jingle [jingling jingled]

jirarf — giraffe
jittery
Jluy — July
job jobless
jockey jockeys
jodhpurs
jog [jogging jogged]
join [joining joined] joiner
joint jointly
joke [joking joked] joker
jokingly
jolly jollier jolliest
jolt [jolting jolted]
joos — deuce *[card]
— juice *[drink]
josel — jostle
jostle [jostling jostled]
jot [jotting jotted]
journal journalism
journalist
journey
[journeys journeying journeyed]
joust [jousting jousted]
jowst — joust
joy joyful joyfully
joyn — join
joynt — joint
joyride [joyriding]

jubilant
jubilee
judge [judging judged]
judgement
judo
juel — duel
jug
juggernaut
juggle [juggling juggled]
juggler
juice *[drink] deuce *[card]
juicy juicier juiciest
jujitsu
July
jumble [jumbling jumbled]
jumbo jet
jump [jumping jumped]
jumper
jumpy jumpier jumpiest
juncshun — junction
junction
June *[month] dune *[sand]
jungle jungly
junior
junk
junkshun — junction
junyer — junior
Jupiter

jurnal	journal	justification	
jurney	journey	justify [justifies justifying justified]	
juror		justiss	justice
jursey	jersey	jut [jutting jutted]	
jury juries		juvenile	
juse	juice *[drink]	juwel	jewel *[gem]
	Jews *[people]	Juze	Jews *[people]
just justly			juice *[drink]
justice			

Check out C
as well

kab	cab
kabbige	cabbage
kafé	café
kage	cage
kaki	khaki
kalculate	calculate
kalculater	calculator
kaleidoscope	
kalender	calendar
kalidoscope	kaleidoscope
kame	came
kamp	camp
kan	can
kangaroo	**kangaroos**
kanoo	canoe
kapchur	capture
karatee	karate
karaoke	
karate	
kareer	career *[job]
karet	carat *[gold]
	carrot *[veg]
karioke	karaoke
karki	khaki
karnival	carnival
kart [karting]	
kasett	cassette
kaution	caution

kave	cave
kayak [kayaking]	
keal	keel
kean	keen
keap	keep
kebab	
kechup	ketchup
kee	key *[lock]
	quay *[dock]
keel [keeling keeled]	
keen keenly keenness	
keep keeper keepsake	
[keeping kept]	
keesh	quiche
keg	
kelidoscope	kaleidoscope
kemist	chemist
kennel	
kept	
kerb *[edge]	**curb** *[stop]
kernel *[seed]	**colonel** *[army]
kestrel	
ketchup	
kettle kettledrum	
key *[lock]	**quay** *[dock]
keyboard keyhole keypad	
khaki	
kibab	kebab

kic   kick

kichen   kitchen

kick [kicking kicked]

kick-off   kick-start

kid   [kidding kidded]

kidnap   kidnapper
   [kidnapping kidnapped]

kidney   kidneys

kight   kite

kik   kick

kill [killing killed]

killd   killed

killer

kiln

kilo   ~byte ~gram

kilo   ~metre ~watt

kilt [kilted]

kind   kindly   kindness

kindergarten

kind-hearted

king   kingdom

kingfisher

king-size   king-sized

kiosk

kipper

kirb   curb *[stop]
          kerb *[edge]

kiss [kisses kissing kissed]

kit *[gear]   kite *[sky]

kitchen

kite

kitten

kiwi

Kleenex™

kleptomania   kleptomaniac

klorafill   chlorophyll

knack

knackered

knave *[Jack]   nave *[church]

knead *[dough]   kneed *[knee]
               need *[must
                   have]

knee [knees kneeing kneed]

kneed *[knee]   knead *[dough]
             need *[have to]

kneel [kneeling knelt]

knew *[fact]   new *[not old]

knickers

knick-knack

knife   knives
  [knifes knifing knifed]

knight *[sir]   night *[dark]

knit *[needles]   nit *[hair]
             night *[dark]

knob   knobbly   knobblier

knock [knocking knocked]

knock-kneed

knollage   knowledge

knot *[tie]   not *[no]

knotty

know *[fact]   no *[not]

know [knowing knew known]

knowingly

knowledge   knowledgeable

knowledgeably

known

knuckle   knuckles

  [knuckling knuckled]

koala bear

kollekshun   collection

Koran

kore   core *[centre]

            corps *[army]

korgi   corgi

koridor   corridor

korps   corpse

kort   caught *[ball]

            court *[law]

Kouran   Koran

krate   crate

krater   crater

krave   crave

krew   crew

krews   crews *[teams]

            cruise *[trip]

krismus   Christmas

Check out
ch as well

kung fu

kurb   curb *[stop]

            kerb *[edge]

kurnel   kernel *[seed]

            colonel *[army]

kwack   quack

kwestshun   question

kwestshunaire questionnaire

kwick   quick

kwiert   quiet

Check out
qu as well

L-plate

labals   labels

label

laber   labour

laboratory   laboratories

laborious   laboriously

labour [labouring laboured]

labourer

Labour Party

Labrador

lace [lacing laced]   lacy

lack [lacking lacked]

lacquer

lacrosse

lad

ladder

laden

ladle [ladling ladled]

lady   ladies

ladybird

laff   laugh

lag [lagging lagged]

lager *[beer]   larger *[size]

laid

lain *[down]   lane *[path]

lair *[den]   layer *[cover]

lak   lack

lake   lakeside

laker   lacquer

lakross   lacrosse

lamb

lame   lamely   lameness

lament [lamenting lamented]

lamp   lampshade

land [landing landed]

land ~lady ~lord ~mark

land ~mine ~slide

Land Rover™

landscape [landscaping landscaped]

lane *[path]   lain *[down]

language

langwij   language

lanky   lankier   lankiest

lantern

lap [lapping lapped]

lapel

lapse [lapsing lapsed]

laptop

larder

larf   laugh

large   largely   largeness

larger *[bigger]   lager *[beer]

largest

larj   large

lark [larking larked]

larva *[insect]   lava *[rock]

larvae

lase   lace *[shoes]

laze *[relax]

laser

lash [lashing lashed]

lash   lashes

lass   lassie   lasses

lasso lassos

last [lasting lasted]

lastly

lasue   lasso

latch [latches latched]

late   lately   lateness

latecomer

later *[after]   latter *[last]

latest

Latin

latitude

latter *[last]   later *[after]

latter   latterly

lauf   laugh

laugh [laughing laughed]

laughable   laughingly

laught   laughed

laughter

launch

[launches launching launched]

launder [laundered]

launderette   laundry

lava *[rock]   larva *[insect]

lavatory   lavatories

lavender

law   lawyer

lawful   lawfully

lawless   lawlessness

lawn   lawnmower

lay [laying laid]

lay   ~about ~man ~out

layer *[cover]   lair *[den]

laze *[relax]   lace *[shoes]

laze [lazing lazed]

lazer   laser

lazy   lazier   laziest

lead *[metal]   led *[took]

lead   leaded   leaden

lead [leading led]

leader   leadership

leaf   leaves   leafy

leaflet

league

leaisure   leisure

leak *[hole]   leek *[veg]

   [leaking leaked]

leakage

leaky   leakier leakiest

lean [leaning leaned leant]

lean leaner leanest

leant	lent
*[past of lean]	*[past of lend]
	Lent *[before Easter]

leap [leaping leapt leaped]

leapfrog

learn [learning learnt learned]

lease [leasing leased]

least

leather leathery

leave [leaving left]

leaves

leccher	lecture

lectern

lecture [lecturing lectured]

lecturn	lectern
led *[guided]	lead *[metal]
leding	leading

ledge

lee ~ward ~way

Leebra	Libra
leece	lease

leech leeches

leed	lead
leef	leaf
leeg	league
leek *[veg]	leak *[hole]

leer [leering leered]

left left-handed

leftenant	lieutenant

leftovers

leg [legging legged]

legal legally

legalise [legalising legalised]

legend legendary

legibility legibly

legible

legislation

legitimate legitimately

leisure leisurely

lej	ledge
lejion	legion

lemon lemonade

lend [lending lent] lender

lene	lean

length ~ways ~wise

lengthen [lengthening lengthened]

lengthy lengthier lengthiest

lenient leniently

lens lenses

lent *[past of lend]

Lent	leant
*[before Easter]	*[past of lean]

lentil

Leo

leopard

leotard

lepard   leopard

leper   leprosy

lept   leapt

lerch   lurch

lerk   lurk

lern   learn

lesher   leisure

less   lesser   least

lessen *[reduce] [lessening lessened]

lesson *[class]

let [letting let]

lethal   lethally

lethargic

lether   leather

letiss   lettuce

letter   lettering

lettuce

leukaemia

level [levelling levelled]

lever

liable

liaise [liaising liaised]

liaison

liar *[lies]   lyre *[music]

liase   liaise

libel

liberal   liberally

Liberal Democrat Party

liberate [liberating liberated]

liberty   liberties

Libra

libral   liberal

librarian

library   libraries

librury   library

lice

licence *[document]

license *[allow] [licensing licensed]

lichen

lick [licking licked]

licker   liquor

lickoriss   liquorice

lid   lidded

lide   lied

lie [lies lying lied]

liebraree   library

lier   leer

lieutenant

life   lives

life   ~belt ~boat ~buoy

life   ~less ~like ~line ~long

life   ~span ~style ~time

life-threatening

lift [lifting lifted]

light [lighting lit]

light ~house ~weight

light lighter lightest

lighten [lightening lightened]

lightening *[make lighter]

lightly lightness

lightning *[flash]

liing lying

like [liking liked]

likeable

likely likeness

liken [likening likened]

likewise

likwid liquid

lilac

lily lilies

limb [limbed]

lime ~light ~stone

limerick

limit [limiting limited]

limitation

limitless

limousine

limozeen limousine

limp [limping limped]

limpet

linch lynch

line [lining lined]

linear

linen

linesman

linger [lingering lingered]

linguist

lining

link [linking linked]

links *[joins]   lynx *[animal]

linoleum lino

lion lioness lionesses

lip lip-read

lipstick

liquid

liquidise liquidiser
    [liquidising liquidised]

liquor

liquorice

lirch   lurch

lire   liar *[tells lies]

   lyre *[music]

liric   lyric

lisen   listen

lisence   licence
      *[document]

   license *[allow]

lison   listen

lisp [lisping lisped]

lissen   listen

list

listen [listening listened]

litel   little

liten   lighten

literacy   literate

literal   literally

literature

litewait   lightweight

litly   lightly

litning   lightning

litrcy   literacy

litre *[measurement]

litter *[rubbish] [littering littered]

little   littler   littlest

littrit   literate

live [living lived]

livelihood

lively   livelier   liveliest

liver

livestock

livid

lizard

llama

load [loading loaded]

loaf *[bread]   loaves

loaf *[laze] [loafing loafed]

loan *[lend]   lone *[alone]

    [loaning loaned]

loathe [loathing loathed]

loathsome

lob [lobbing lobbed]

lobster

local   locally

locality   localities

locamotiv   locomotive

locate [located]   location

loch *[lake]

Loch Ness Monster

lock *[door, canal] [locking locked]

locket

locomotion   locomotive

loct   locked

locust

lodge [lodging lodged]

lodgings

lods   loads

loft

loftier loftiest

log [logging logged]

loge   lodge

logic   logical   logically

logo   logos

loiter [loitering loitered]

lojic   logic

lok   loch *[lake]

          lock *[door]

lokal   local

lokalitee   locality

lokate   locate

lokomoshun   locomotion

lokust   locust

loll [lolling lolled]

lollipop   lolly   lollies

lone *[alone]   loan *[lend]

lonely   lonelier   loneliest

loner

long [longing longed]

longer   longest

longingly

longitude

look [looking looked]

look   ~alike ~out

loom [looming loomed]

loonatic   lunatic

loop [looping looped]

loophole

loose *[not tight]   lose *[not win]

loose   looser   loosest

loosely   looseness

loosen [loosening loosened]

loot *[goods]   lute *[musical]
   [looting looted]

lopsided

lord   lordly

Lords [the]

loreful   lawful

lorless   lawless

lornch   launch

lorndree   laundry

lornmower ·   lawnmower

lorry   lorries

lose *[not win] loose *[not tight]
   [losing lost]

loshun   lotion

loss   losses

lost

lot

lotion

lottery   lotteries

lotto

lottree   lottery

loud   louder   loudest

loudly   loudness

loud   ~mouth ~speaker

lounge [lounging lounged]

lousy   lousier   lousiest

lout   loutish

lovable

love [loving loved]   lover

love   ~sick ~song

lovely   lovelier   loveliest

loving   lovingly

low   lower   lowest
low   ~lands ~ness
lowd   loud
lower [lowering lowered]
lowly lowlier lowliest
lownge   lounge
lowsy   lousy
lowt   lout
loyal   loyally
loyalty   loyalties
loyer   lawyer
loyter   loiter
lozenge
lrst   last
luck lucky luckier luckiest
lucksurius   luxurious
lucksury   luxury
lucly   luckily
ludicrous   ludicrously
lug [lugging lugged]
luggage
luggige   luggage
lukeemia   leukaemia
lukewarm
lull [lulling lulled]
lullaby   lullabies
lumber [lumbering lumbered]
lumberjack

lume   loom
luminous
lump [lumping lumped]
lumpy   lumpier   lumpiest
lunacy   lunatic
lunar
lunasy   lunacy
lunch   lunches
lunchtime
luner   lunar
lung
lunge [lunging lunged]
lurch [lurches lurching lurched]
lure [luring lured]
lurk [lurking lurked]
lurn   learn
luscious
luse   loose *[not tight]
                lose *[not win]
lush   lusher   lushest
lushus   luscious
lusse   loose
lussen   loosen
lust   lustful   lustfully
lute *[music]   loot *[goods]
luvly   lovely
luxurious   luxuriously
luxury   luxuries

ly	lie

lyase	liaise
lybraree	library
lyce	lice
Lycra™	

lyer	liar *[tells lies]
	lyre *[music]
lying	
lynch [lynching lynched]	
lyon	lion
lyre *[music]	liar *[lies]
lyrics lyrical	

ma'am

macaroni

macaw

Mach   March

mach   match

machete

machine   machinery

machine-gun

machure   mature

mack   make

mackerel

mackintosh   mackintoshes

macor   macaw

mad *[crazy]   made *[built]

          maid *[girl]

mad   madder   maddest

mad   madly   madness

madam

madden [maddening maddened]

made *[built]   mad *[crazy]

          maid *[girl]

maed   made

maer   mayor

maffs   maths

magazine

mager   major

magestic   majestic

magesty   majesty

maggot

magic   magical   magically

magician

magistrate

magnesium

magnet   magnetic

magnificent   magificently

magnify

   [magnifies magnifying magnified]

magnification

magnifying glass

magots   maggots

magpie

mahogany

maid *[girl]   made *[built, did]

mail *[post]   male *[man]

   [mailing mailed]

maim [maiming maimed]

main *[chief]   mane *[hair]

mainly

maintain [maintaining maintained]

maintenance

mait   mate

maize *[corn]   maze *[lost]

majestic   majestically

majesty   majesties

majic   magic

majishun   magician

majistrate   magistrate

major

majority

mak   make

makaroni   macaroni

make [making made]   maker

make-believe

making

makintosh   mackintosh

maksimum   maximum

malaria

male *[man]   mail *[post]

malicious   maliciously

mall *[shops]   maul *[hurt]

mallet

malnewtrishun malnutrition

malnutrition

mame   maim

mammal

mammoth

man [manning manned]

man   ~eater ~kind ~power

manage   manageable

  [managing managed]

management

manager *[boss]   manger *[box]

mandarin

mane *[hair]   main *[chief]

maner   manner

manewer   manure

mange   mangy

manged   managed

manger *[box]   manager *[boss]

mangle [mangled]

mango   mangoes

manhandle

  [manhandling manhandled]

mania

maniac *[mad person]

manic *[excited]

manicure

manipulate

  [manipulating manipulated]

manipulative

maniqure   manicure

manly   manlier   manliest

manliness

manner *[way]   manor *[house]

manners

manor *[house]   manner *[way]

manshun   mansion

mansion

manslaughter

manslorter   manslaughter

mantelpiece

manual   manually

manufacture [manufactured]

manufacturer

manure

manuscript

many   more   most

Maori

map [mapping mapped]

marathon

marble

march *[walk] marches
  [marching marched]

March *[month]

mare *[horse]   mayor *[city]

margarine

margin

marige   marriage

marigold

marina *[harbour]

marine *[army, sea]

marjarin   margarine

marjin   margin

mark [marking marked]

marker

market [marketing marketed]

markey   marquee

marksman

marmalade

maroon [marooned]

marquee

marreid   married

marriage

marrow

marry [marries marrying married]

Mars   Martian

marsh   marshy

Marshan   Martian

marshine   machine

marshmallow

marsipan   marzipan

marst   mast

martial arts

Martian

martyr   martyrdom

marune   maroon

marvel [marvelling marvelled]

marvellous   marvellously

marys   marries

marzipan

masaker   massacre

masarge   massage

mascara

mascot

masculine

mash [mashes mashing mashed]

mashetee   machete

mashine   machine

mask *[cover]   masque *[ball]
  [masking masked]

maskot   mascot

maskulin   masculine

mass   masses

massacre [massacring massacred]

massage [massaging massaged]

massive   massively

mast

master [mastering mastered]

master   ~mind ~piece

masterful   masterfully

mastermind [masterminded]

mat *[rug]   mate *[friend]
                matt *[dull]

matador

match   matches
  [matching matched]

match   ~box ~less ~maker

mate [mating mated]

matedor   matador

material   materialistic

maternal   maternally

maternity

mathematician

mathematics   mathematical

maths

matinée

matiriel   material

matrimony

matrix   matrices

matron   matronly

matt *[dull]   mat *[rug]

matter [mattered]

matting

mattress   mattresses

mature   maturely   maturity
  [maturing matured]

maturnal   maternal

maul *[hurt]   mall *[shops]
  [mauling mauled]

mauve

maveles   marvellous

maximum

may *[perhaps]   May *[month]

maybe

mayday *[SOS]   May Day
                *[1st May]

mayde   made *[built]
                maid *[girl]

maym   maim

mayonnaise

mayor *[city]   mare *[horse]

mayoress

mayt   mate

maze *[lost]   maize *[corn]

135

me

meadow

meal ~time

mean *[average, imply]

  [meaning meant]

mean   meaner   meanest

mean *[nasty]

meaning   ~ful ~fully ~less

meanly   meanness

meant

meantime

meanwhile

measles

measurable

measure   measurement

  [measuring measured]

meat *[flesh]   meet *[hello]

meaty   meatier   meatiest

mecanic   mechanic

Mecca

mechanic   mechanical

mechanically

mechanism

medal *[award]   meddle *[pry]

medallion

medallist

meddle *[pry]   medal *[award]

  [meddling meddled]

meddow   meadow

media

median

medical   medically

medication

medicine   medicinal

medieval

meditate   meditation

  [meditating meditated]

Mediterranean

medium

meek   meeker   meekest

meekly

meet *[hello]   meat *[flesh]

  [meeting met]

mega ~byte ~phone

megafone   megaphone

Meka   Mecca

mekanic   mechanic

melen   melon

melon

melt [melting melted]

member ~ship

Member of Parliament

membrane

memo

memoirs

memorable   memorably

memorial

memorise [memorising memorised]

memory memories

men

menace [menacing menaced]

menay   many

mend [mending mended]

meniss   menace

menshun   mention

mental mentally

mentality

mention [mentioning mentioned]

menu menus

meny   many

merang   meringue

merchant

merciful mercifully

merciless mercilessly

mercury *[metal]

Mercury *[planet]

mercy mercies

merder   murder

merge [merging merged]

meringue

merit [meriting merited]

mermaid

mermer   murmur

merry merrier merriest

mersiless   merciless

mesels   measles

mesh [meshes meshed]

meshurabul   measurable

meshure   measure

mesige   message

mess [messing messed]

message messaging

messenger

messtak   mistake

messy messier messiest

met

metafor   metaphor

metal metallic

metaphor

meteor meteorite

meter *[gas]   metre *[length]

method

methodical methodically

methylated spirits meths

metior   meteor

metre *[length]   meter *[gas]

metric

mew [mewing mewed]

mewchal   mutual

mewseum   museum

mewsik   music

mewsishan   musician

137

mewtinear   mutineer

Mey   May

miaow [miaowing miaowed]

mice

micro   ~chip ~light

micro   ~phone ~scope

micro   ~scopic ~wave

midday   midnight

middle

Middle East

midge

midget

midia   media

midian   median

midium   medium

midst *[middle]   mist *[fog]

                 missed *[let go]

midul   middle

midwife   midwives

miget   midget

might   mite *[insect]

  *[strength, may]

mighty   mightier   mightiest

migraine

migrate   migration

  [migrating migrated]

migt   might

mike

mikroskope   microscope

mild   milder   mildest

mildew

mildly   mildness

mile   mileage   milestone

military

milk [milking milked]

milk   ~man ~shake

milky   milkier   milkiest

Milky Way

mill [milling milled]   miller

millennium

milligram   millilitre

millimetre

million   ~aire ~airess

millionth

millipede

mime [miming mimed]

mimic [mimicking mimicked]

mince

mind [minding minded]

mindless   mindlessly

mine [mining mined]

mine   ~field ~sweeper

miner *[coal]   minor *[lesser]

mineral

minet   minute

mingle [mingling mingled]

mini ~beast ~bus ~skirt

miniature

minimum

minister

ministry   ministries

mink

minnow

minor *[lesser]   miner *[coal]

minority

minstrel

mint

minus

minut   minute

minute *[time]

minute *[small]   minutely

miracle

miraculous   miraculously

mirage

mirarj   mirage

mirge   merge

mirmade   mermaid

mirmer   murmur

mirror

misbehave   misbehaviour
  [misbehaving misbehaved]

miscarriage

miscellaneous

mischief   mischievous

mise   mice

miser   miserly

miserable   miserably

misery   miseries

misfire [misfiring misfired]

misfit

misfortune

misgide   misguide

misgivings

misheard

mishun   mission

misjudge [misjudging misjudged]

mislay [mislaying mislaid]

mislead [misleading misled]

misplace [misplaced]

misprint

misrabull   miserable

miss [missing missed]

missed *[failed]   mist *[fog]

missile

missing

mission

missionary   missionaries

misspell [misspelling misspelt]

mist *[fog]   missed *[failed]

mistake
  [mistaking mistook mistaken]

misterius   mysterious

Check out
my as well

mistic	mystic
mistifyed	mystified
mistletoe	
mistook	
mistreat	mistreatment
[mistreating mistreated]	
mistress	mistresses
mistrust [mistrusted]	
mistry	mystery
misty	mistier mistiest
misunderstand	
[misunderstanding misunderstood]	
misuse [misusing misused]	
mite *[insect]	might *[strength, may]
mith	myth
mity	mighty
mix [mixing mixed]	mixture
miy	my
mizer	miser
mizeree	misery
mizrabul	miserable
mnemonic	
moan *[groan]	mown *[grass]
moat	

mob [mobbing mobbed]

mobile phone

mobility

mock [mocking mocked]

mockery

mode

model [modelling modelled]

modem

moderate   moderately

modern

modernise   modernisation
  [modernising modernised]

modest   modestly   modesty

modurn   modern

moist   moisture

moisten [moistening moistened]

molar

molde   mould

mole   molehill

molecule   molecular

molte   moult

molten

moment   momentous

momentum

monaky   monarchy

monarch

monarchy   monarchies

monastery   monastries

monastic

Monday

money [moneyed]

mongoose

mongrel

monie   money

monitor [monitoring monitored]

monk

monkey

monologue

monopolise

  [monopolising monopolised]

monopoly

monotonous   monotony

monotonously

monsieur

monsoon

monster   monstrous

monstrosity   monstrosities

monsyer   monsieur

month   monthly

monument   monumental

mony   money

moo [mooing mooed]

mood *[temper]   mooed *[cow]

moody   moodier   moodiest

moon   ~beam ~light

moon   ~lit ~shine

moor *[land]   more *[greater]

moor *[boat] [mooring moored]

moorhen

moose *[deer]   mousse *[pud]

mooslee   muesli

moove   move

moovee   movie

mop *[clean] [mopping mopped]

mope *[do nothing] [moping moped]

moped *[bike]

mopped *[cleaned]

moral *[good] **morally**

morale *[confidence]

morality

morbid   morbidly

more *[greater]   moor *[land]

moreover

morgige   mortgage

morl   maul *[hurt]

         mall *[shops]

mornful   mournful

morning

Morse code

morsel

mortal   mortality

mortally

mortar

mortgage [mortgaged]

mortuary

mosaic

moshun   motion

mosk   mosque

moskito   mosquito

mosque

mosquito   mosquitoes

moss   mosses   mossy

most   mostly

motel

moth   motheaten

mother   motherhood

motherly

motion   motionless

motivate   motivator

   [motivating motivated]

motivation

motive

motor [motoring motored]

motor   ~bike ~boat

motor   ~cycle ~cyclist

motor   ~ist ~way

motorised

motto   mottoes

mould [moulding moulded]

mouldy   mouldier   mouldiest

moult [moulting moulted]

mound

mount [mounting mounted]

mountain   mountainous

mountaineer   mountaineering

mourn *[sad]   morn *[a.m.]

   [mourning mourned]

mournful   mournfully

mouse   mice

mousse *[pud]   moose *[deer]

moustache

mousy

mouth   mouthful

move [moving moved]

movement

mow [mowing mowed mown]

mower

mown *[grass]   moan *[groan]

mownd   mound

mowntain   mountain

Mowri   Maori

mowse   mouse

mowth   mouth

moyst   moist

much

muck [mucking mucked]

mucky   muckier   muckiest

mud

muddle [muddling muddled]

muddy   muddier   muddiest

muing	mewing	munkey	monkey
muel	mule	munsh	munch
muesli		muny	money
muffin		mural	
muffle [muffling muffled]		murang	meringue
mug [mugging mugged]		murcy	mercy
mule		murder [murdering murdered]	
multicoloured		murderer murderess	
multicultural		murderous	
multilingual		murge	merge
multi-millionaire		murky murkier murkiest	
multiple		murmaid	mermaid
multiplication		murmur [murmuring murmured]	
multiply [multiplies]		mursee	mercy
[multiplying multiplied]		mursiful	merciful
multiracial		muscle *[body] mussel *[eat]	
multi-storey		[muscling muscled]	
mum		muscular	
mumble [mumbling mumbled]		museum	
mummy mummies		mushy	
mumps		mushroom	
munch [munching munched]		music musical musically	
munches		musician	
Mundy	Monday	musik	music
mune	moon	musishan	musician
muney	money	musium	museum
mungrel	mongrel	musket musketeer	
munk	monk	Muslim	

mussel *[eat]   muscle *[body]

must   mustn't [must not]

mustard

mustash   moustache

musty   mustier   mustiest

mutant

mute [muted]

mutineer

mutiny   mutinies

mutter [muttering muttered]

muvabul   movable

muve   move

muzzle [muzzling muzzled]

my   myself

myaow   miaow

Check out
mi as well

myld   mild

mynah *[bird]   minor *[lesser]

mysterious   mysteriously

mystery   mysteries

mystify [mystifies]

  [mystifying mystified]

myth   mythical

nacher   nature

nacheral   natural

nag [nagging nagged]

nail [nailing nailed]

nail-biting

nak   knack

naked   nakedness

nale   nail

name [naming named]

nameless   namely

nanny   nannies

nap [napping napped]

napkin

nappy   nappies

narled   gnarled

narrate   narrator

  [narrating narrated]

narration   narrative

narrow   narrower   narrowest

narrowly

narrow-minded

nasal

nash   gnash

nashun   nation

nashunality   nationality

nasty   nastier   nastiest

nat   gnat

nation   nationwide

national

National Health Service

nationality   nationalities

native

Nativity

natural   naturally

naturalist

nature

naughtier   naughtiest

naughty

nausea   nauseous

naval *[navy]   navel *[tummy]

navee   navy

navel *[tummy]   naval *[navy]

navey   navy

navigate   navigator

  [navigating navigated]

navigation

navul   naval *[navy]
                navel *[tummy]

navy   navies

naw   gnaw *[bite]
                nor *[neither]

nawr   now

naybor   neighbour

naytiv   native

nazel   nasal

Nazi   Nazism

nead	knead *[dough]
	need *[must have]
	kneed *[with knee]
neadle	needle
near nearer nearest	
near nearby nearly	
neat neater neatest	
neatly neatness	
necessarily	
necessary	
neck necklace	
necst	next
nectar nectarine	
nee	knee
need *[must have] knead *[dough]	
needle [needling needled]	
needless needlessly	
needy needier neediest	
neel	kneel
neer	near
neese	niece
nefew	nephew
negative negatively	
neglect neglectful	
[neglecting neglected]	
negotiate [negotiating negotiated]	
neigh [neighing neighed]	

neighbour neighbouring
neighbourhood neighbourly
neither

nek	neck
nekst	next
nelt	knelt
nemonic	mnemonic

neon
nephew

nerse	nurse

nerve nerve-racking
nervous nervously
nervousness nervy

nesessary	necessary

nest [nesting nested]
nestle [nestling nestled]
net *[mesh]   neat *[tidy]
net netball network

netley	neatly

nettle
neuter [neutered]
neutral
never nevertheless
new *[not old]   knew *[fact]
newer newest
newly newness
new ~born ~comer

newclear	nuclear

newcleus	nucleus

Check out
nu as well

newdist	nudist
newgar	nougat
newmerus	numerous
news	~agent ~flash
news	~letter ~paper ~reader
newsons	nuisance
newt	
newtrishun	nutrition
next	
nib	

nibble [nibbling nibbled]

nice *[kind]	niece *[aunt]
nicer nicest nicely	

nick [nicking nicked]

nickers	knickers

nickname [nicknamed]

niece *[aunt]	nice *[kind]
nieghbour	neighbour
nier	near
niese	niece
niet	night
nife	knife
night *[dark]	knight *[man]
night	~club ~dress ~fall

night	~shirt ~time
nightingale	
nightly	
nightmare	nightmarish
nihgt	night
nikname	nickname
nil	
nilon	nylon
nimble nimbly	
nimf	nymph
nine ninth	
nineteen nineteenth	
ninety nineties ninetieth	
ninteen	nineteen

nip [nipping nipped]

nipple	
nirve	nerve
nirvos	nervous
nise	nice *[kind]
nit *[insect]	knit *[wool]

Check out
kn as well

nite	knight *[man]
	night *[dark]
nither	neither
nitrogen	
nitting	knitting

no *[not]*   know *[fact]*

noble nobleman nobility

nobler noblest nobly

nobody

nock   knock

nocturnal

nod [nodding nodded]

noise noiseless noiselessly

noisy noisier noisiest

nollij   knowledge

nomad nomadic

nome   gnome

noncense   nonsense

none *[not any]* nun *[God]*

non-existent

non-fiction

nonsense

non-starter

non-stop

noodle

noon *[midday]*

no one *[not any person]*

noose

noospaper   newspaper

nor *[neither]* gnaw *[bite]*

norghty   naughty

norm

normal normality

normally

Norman Conquest

normly   normally

norsea   nausea

norseus   nauseous

north ~bound north-east

north ~erly ~ern ~erner

North Pole

north ~wards north-west

norty   naughty

nose *[face]*   knows *[fact]*

nosedive [nosedived]

nostril

nosy nosier nosiest

not *[no]*   knot *[tie]*

notch notches

note [noting noted]

note ~book ~card

note ~pad ~paper

nothing nothingness

notice [noticing noticed]

noticeable noticeably

noticeboard

notiss   notice

nought

noun *[word]*   known *[fact]*

nourish nourishment
[nourishing nourished]

novel   novelist

novelty   novelties

November

now   nowadays

nowere   nowhere

nowhere

nowlege   knowledge

nown   known *[fact]

                noun *[word]

nowon   no one

noyse   noise

noze   knows *[fact]

                nose *[face]

nozzle

nuckel   knuckle

nuclear   nuclear power

nucleus   nuclei

nude   nudity

nudge [nudging nudged]

nue   knew *[fact]

                new *[not old]

nues   news

nugget

nuisance

nuj   nudge

numb   numbness

number [numbering numbered]

numeracy

numeral

numerasee   numeracy

numerator

numerical

numerous

numonia   pneumonia

nun *[God]   none *[not any]

nurrish   nourish

nurse [nursing nursed]

nursery   nurseries

nursing home

nurvous   nervous

nurvy   nervy

nut   nutcracker   nutshell

nute   newt

nuter   neuter

nutrition

nutron   neutron

nutty   nuttier   nuttiest

nuzzle [nuzzling nuzzled]

nxte   next

nylon

nymph

oad

ode *[poem]

owed *[money]

oaf   oafish

oak

oan

own *[belongs]

oar

or *[alternative]

ore *[mineral]

oarsman

oasis   oases

oath

obay   obey

obedient   obedience

obediently

obedyans   obedience

obeece   obese

obese   obesity

obey [obeying obeyed]

obidyant   obedient

object   objector

  [objecting objected]

objection   objectionable

objective

objekt   object

obligation

oblige [obliging obliged]

oblong

oblyge   oblige

obnoxious

oboe   oboist

obow   oboe

obscene   obscenely

obscure   obscurity

obseen   obscene

observant   observation

observe   observer

  [observing observed]

obsessed   obsession

obsessive

obskure   obscure

obsolete

obsqure   obscure

obsqurity   obscurity

obstacle

obstinacy

obstinate   obstinately

obstruct   obstruction

  [obstructing obstructed]

obsurd   absurd

obsurve   observe

obtain   obtainable

  [obtaining obtained]

obtuse angle

obvious   obviously

ocashun   occasion

occasional   occasionally

occupation

occupy [occupies]
  [occupying occupied]

occur [occurring occurred]

ocean

ockur   occur

o'clock

octagon   octagonal

octave

octiv   octave

October

octopus   octopuses

ocupashun   occupation

ocupie   occupy

ocur   occur

odd   odder   oddest

oddity   oddities

oddly   oddments

ode *[poem]   owed *[money]

oder   odour

odour   odourless

ods   odds

of *[part]   off *[not on]

ofal   awful

of course

ofen   often

ofense   offence

ofensive   offensive

ofer   offer

off *[not on]   of *[part]

offence

offend [offending offended]

offensive   offensively

offer [offering offered]

offhand

office   officer

official   officially

officious   officiously

offside

offten   often

ofice   office

ofiser   officer

ofishall   official

ofsyd   offside

often

oger   ogre

ogre

Ogst   August

oh *[surprise]   owe *[money]

oil [oiling oiled]

oily   oilier   oiliest

ointment

okcupashun   occupation

Check out
oc as well

okcupyd   occupied

151

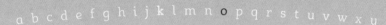

okcur	occur
o'klock	o'clock
oksidise	oxidise
oksygen	oxygen
oktagon	octagon
Oktober	October
oktopus	octopus

old   old-fashioned

Olimpic	Olympic

olive

Olympic Games

omelette

omen

ominous   ominously

omishun	omission

omission

omit [omitting omitted]

omlet	omelette
omminus	ominous
ommit	omit

omnivore   omnivorous

on   ongoing

once *[one time]   wants *[would like]

one *[single]   won *[victory]

one   one-way

oner	owner
onest	honest

onion

online

onlooker

only

onomatopoeia   onomatopoeic

onse	once

onset

onslort	onslaught

onto

onts	once

onward   onwards

onyun	onion

ooze [oozing oozed]

opan	open

open [opening opened]

openly   opener

opera   operatic

operashun	operation

operate   operator
  [operating operated]

opinion   opinionated

oponent	opponent
oposit	opposite

opponent

opporchunity	opportunity

opportunity   opportunities

oppose [opposing opposed]

opposite   opposition

oppress [oppresses]
   [oppressing oppressed]
oppression   oppressor
opra   opera
opropryet   appropriate
opshun   option
opt [opting opted]
optic   optical
optician
optimism   optimistically
optimist   optimistic
option   optional
optishun   optician
opurate   operate
or *[either]   awe *[wonder]
                    oar *[boat]
                    ore *[mineral]
oral *[mouth]   aural *[ear]
orally
orange
orang-utan
orbit [orbiting orbited]
orchard
orchestra   orchestral
orchid
ordeal
order [ordering ordered]
orderly

ordinal number
ordinary   ordinarily
ordnary   ordinary
ordur   order
ore *[mineral]   awe *[wonder]
                    oar *[boat]
                    or *[either]
orfan   orphan
organ   organist
organic   organically
organise   organisation
   [organising organised]
organism
Orgust   August
oriant   orient
oriental
orienteering
origin
original   originally
originality
originate [originating originated]
orijin   origin
orijinal   original
oringe   orange
orkestra   orchestra
orl   all
ornament   ornamental
ornge   orange

153

orphan   orphanage   orphaned

ort   ought

orthodontist

ortistic   autistic

ortum   autumn

oshun   ocean

osmosis

Ostralyer   Australia

ostrich   ostriches

ote   oat

othar   other

otherwise

otter

ouch

ought *[should]

oughtn't *[should not]

oul   owl

ounce

our *[owns]   are *[we are]
                hour *[time]

ourang-outang   orang-utan

ours *[owns]   hours *[time]

ourselves

out   ~back ~break

out   ~board ~burst ~come

out   ~door ~fit ~let ~line

out   ~look ~number ~patient

out   ~right ~set ~side ~skirts

outdo [outdoes]
    [outdoing outdid outdone]

outer space

outrayjus   outrageous

outrageous

outspoken

outstanding

outward   outwardly

outward-bound

outwards

owa   our

oval

ovary   ovaries

ovel   oval

oven   ovenproof

over   ~act ~arm ~board

over   ~cast ~coat ~come

over   ~do ~due ~flow

over   ~grown ~hang ~hear

over   ~heat ~joyed ~land

over   ~lap ~look ~seas

over   ~time ~weight

overtake [overtaking]
    [overtook overtaken]

overwait   overweight

overwelm   overwhelm

overwhelm [overwhelming]
    [overwhelmed]

ovursee   **oversee**

ow *[pain]*

owe *[money]*   **oh** *[surprise]*
    [owing owed]

owed *[money]*   **ode** *[poem]*

owl   **owlish**

own [owning owned]

owner

ownly   **only**

owtberst   **outburst**

owtdoor   **outdoor**

Check out
out as well

owter   **outer**

ox   **oxen**   **oxtail**

oxygen

oyel   **oil**

oyntment   **ointment**

oyster

ozone layer

pace [pacing paced]

pacemaker

pack [packing packed]

package

packed *[case]   pact *[deal]

packet

pact *[deal]   packed *[case]

pad *[cloth]   paid *[money]
   [padding padded]

paddle [paddling paddled]

paddock

pade   paid

padlock [padlocked]

pagan

page

paid

pain *[ow!]   pane *[glass]

pain ~free ~killer ~less

painful   painfully

paint [painting painted]

pair *[two]   pare *[trim]
                pear *[fruit]

paj   page

paket   packet

palace   palatial

pale *[colour]   pail *[bucket]

paler   palest

paliss   palace

palm   palmist

Palm Sunday

pamflet   pamphlet

pamper [pampered]

pamphlet

pan   pancake

pane *[glass]   pain *[ow!]

panel

panic   panic-stricken

panicked   panicking   panicky

panorama   panoramic

pansy   pansies

pant [panting panted]

panther

pantomime

paper ~back ~work

papier-mâché

parachute [parachuting parachuted]

parade [parading paraded]

paradise

paragraph

parallel   parallelogram

paralyse [paralysed]

parashoot   parachute

parasite

parcel

parched

pardon [pardoned]

parellel   parallel

parent

park [parking parked]

parlement   parliament

parliament

parm   palm

parrot

parsel   parcel

parsley

parsnip

parst   past

part [parting parted]

parth   path

partly

partner

party   parties

pashence   patience
                 *[calmness]
                 patients
                 *[doctor's]

pashent   patient

pass [passing passed]

pass   passport   password

passage   passageway

passed *[over]   past *[time]

passenger

passige   passage

past *[time]   passed *[over]

pasta

pastel

pastime

pastry   pastries

pat [patting patted]

patch   patches [patching patched]

path

pathetic   pathetically

patience *[calmness]

patients *[ill people]

patient   patiently

patio

patriotic

patrol [patrolling patrolled]

pattern [patterned]

pause *[wait]   paws *[feet]
   [pausing paused]

pave [paving paved]

pavement

paw *[foot]   poor *[needy]
   [pawing pawed]   pore *[skin, scan]
                    pour *[tip]

pawch   porch

paws *[feet]   pause *[stop]

pawshun   portion

pay [paying paid]

payment

paynt   paint

pea

peace *[calm]   piece *[part]

peaceful   peacefully

peach   peaches

peacock

peak *[top]   peek *[glance]
  [peaking peaked]

peal *[bells]   peel *[skin]

peanut

pear *[fruit]   pare *[trim]

pearl *[gem]   purl *[knit]

pearly

peasant

pebble   pebbly

peculiar   peculiarity

pedal [pedalling pedalled]

pedestrian

peece   peace *[calm]
         piece *[part]

peech   peach

peek *[glance]   peak *[top]
  [peeking peeked]

peel *[skin]   peal *[bells]
  [peeling peeled]

peep [peeping peeped]

peer [peering peered]

peeriodd   period

peetza   pizza

peg [pegging pegged]

peice   peace *[calm]
         piece *[part]

pekuliar   peculiar

pelican   pelican crossing

pelt [pelting pelted]

pen

penalty   penalties

pence *[money]   pens *[ink]

pencil [pencilled]

penguin

pengwin   penguin

penicillin

peninsula

penisillin   penicillin

penknife   penknives

penniless

pens *[ink]   pence *[money]

penshun   pension

pensil   pencil

pension   pensioner

pentagon

pentathlon

people

peple   people

pepper   peppery

peppermint

pepule   people

per cent percentage

perception perceptive

perch [perches perching perched]

perchase   purchase

percussion

perfect [perfected]

perfection perfectly

perform performance

  [performing performed]

perfume

perhaps

perimeter

period

perish [perished]

perm [permed]

permanent permanently

permission

permit [permitting permitted]

perpendicular

perple   purple

perposs   purpose

perr   purr

perse   purse

persecute [persecuting persecuted]

persenly   personally

persevere perseverance

  [persevering persevered]

persist [persisted]

persistent persistently

person personal personally

personality personalities

persuade [persuading persuaded]

persuasion

persuasive

persue   pursue

persute   pursuit

perswade   persuade

pesant   peasant

pessimism

pessimist pessimistic

pest pesticide

pester [pestering pestered]

pet [petting petted]

petal

petishun   petition

petition

petrify [petrifies]

  [petrifying petrified]

petrol

petticoat

pew

pewpil   pupil

phantom

Pharaoh

phase

pheasant

phenomenal phenomenon

phew *[sigh]   few *[not many]

philosopher

phoan   phone
                    *[telephone]

phobia

phone [phoning phoned]

phonics

photo ~copier

photocopy [photocopied]

photograph [photographed]

photographer photography

photosynthesis

phrase

physical physically

physics

piano pianist

piccher   picture

pich   pitch

pick [picking picked]

pick ~axe ~pocket

pickle [pickled]

picnic picnickers
  [picnicking picnicked]

picture [pictured]

pie

piece *[part]   peace *[calm]
  [piecing pieced]

pieneer   pioneer

pierce [piercing pierced]

pierse   pierce

pig piglet

pigeon pigeonhole

piggy ~back ~bank

pigheaded

pigsty pigsties

pijarmas   pyjamas

pik   pick

pikcher   picture

pile [piling piled]

pilfer [pilfering pilfered]

pilgrim pilgrimage

pill

pillar pillarbox

pillow pillowcase

pilon   pylon

pilot [piloting piloted]

pimple pimply

pin *[point]   pine *[tree, sad]

pinch [pinches pinching pinched]

pine [pining pined]

pineapple

ping-pong

pink pinker pinkest

pint

pioneer [pioneering]

pip *[seed]

pipe *[tube] [piping piped]

piramid   pyramid

pirate   piracy

pirote   pirate

Pisces

pistil *[flower]

pistol *[gun]

pitch   pitches [pitched]

pithon   python

pity [pities pitying pitied]

pixie

pizza

place [placing placed]

plaed   played

plague [plaguing plagued]

plain   plainly

plait *[hair]   plate *[dish]
   [plaiting plaited]

plan [planning planned]

plane *[aircraft]   plain *[basic]

planet   planetary

plank

plant [planting planted]

plasis   places

plaster [plastering plastered]

plastic

Plasticine™

plat   plait

plate *[dish]   plait *[hair]

platform

play [playing played]

play   ~ground ~group ~mate

play   ~school ~script ~time

playd   played

playful   playfully

plead [pleading pleaded]

pleasant   pleasantly

please [pleasing pleased]

pleasure   pleasurable

pleat [pleated]

pledge [pledging pledged]

pleeze   please

plenty   plentiful

plezant   pleasant

plezure   pleasure

plight *[state]   polite *[good]

plimsolls

plite   plight *[state]
            polite *[good]

plod [plodding plodded]

plot [plotting plotted]

plough [ploughing ploughed]

plow   plough

pluck [plucked]

plucky   pluckier   pluckiest

plug [plugging plugged]

plum *[fruit]   plume *[feather]

plumber   plumbing

plummer   plumber

plump   plumper   plumpest

plunder [plundered]

plunge [plunging plunged]

plus

plyte   plight

pneumonia

poach   poacher

[poaching poached]

poak   poke

poar   paw *[foot]

poor *[needy]

pore *[skin, scan]

pour *[liquid]

poch   poach

pocket   pocketful

[pocketing pocketed]

pod

podgy   podgier   podgiest

poem

poepel   people

poet   poetic   poetical

poetry

pogy   podgy

point [pointing pointed]

pointless   pointlessly

poise [poised]

poison   poisonous

[poisoning poisoned]

poitree   poetry

poke [poking poked]

poker

poket   pocket

pokey

polar   polar bear

pole *[stick]   poll *[vote]

pole vault

polees   police

poler   polar

police   ~man ~woman

policy   policies

poligon   polygon

polish [polishing polished]

poliss   police

polite *[good]   plight *[state]

politely   politeness

politheen   polythene

political   politician

politics

politishun   politician

poll *[vote]   pole *[stick]

pollen

pollinate [pollinated]

pollination

pollute [polluting polluted]

pollution

polo

poloot   pollute

poltry   poultry

polygon

polyte   polite

polythene

pome   poem

pompous   pompously

pond

ponder [pondered]

ponee   pony

pony   ponies

ponytail

poodle

pool *[water]   pull *[move]

pool *[collect] [pooling pooled]

poor *[needy]   paw *[foot]

              pore *[skin, scan]

              pour *[liquid]

poorer   poorest   poorly

pop [popping popped]

popcorn

Pope [the]

poplar *[tree]   popular *[liked]

poppy   poppies

popular   popularity

populated   population

por   paw *[foot]

             poor *[needy]

             pore *[skin, scan]

             pour *[liquid]

porch   porches

porcupine

pore *[skin, scan]   paw *[foot]

   [poring pored]   poor *[needy]

               pour *[liquid]

pork

pornch   paunch

porridge

porse   pause *[stop]

             paws *[feet]

porshun   portion

port   portable

porter

portion

portrait

poscher   posture

pose [posing posed]

posession   possession

posh   posher   poshest

poshun   potion

posishun   position

position [positioned]

positive   positively

possess

  [possesses possessing possessed]

possession

possessive   possessively

possibility   possibilities

possible   possibly

post [posting posted]

post   ~box ~card ~code

post   ~man ~mark ~office

postage   postage stamp

postal   postal order

poster

postige   postage

post-mortem

postpone [postponing postponed]

posture

posy   posies

posytiv   positive

pot [potting potted]

pot-belly

pot   ~hole ~holing

potato   potatoes

potenshul   potential

potential   potentially

potion

potter [pottering pottered]

pottery   potteries

pottry   pottery

pouch   pouches

poultry

pounce [pouncing pounced]

pound [pounding pounded]

pour *[liquid]   paw *[foot]

  [pouring poured] poor *[needy]

                pore *[skin, scan]

pout [pouting pouted]

poverty

powch   pouch

powder [powdered]   powdery

power [powered] powerless

powerful   powerfully

power station

pownd   pound

pownse   pounce

powt   pout

powur   power

poynt   point

poyson   poison

poze   pose

practical   practically

practice *[way]

practise *[do] [practising practised]

praer   prayer

praise [praising praised]

praktikal   practical

pram

prance [prancing pranced]

prank

pranse   prance

prawn

pray *[to God]   prey *[hunt]
   [praying prayed]

prayer

prayse   praise

preach [preaches]
   [preaching preached]

precarious   precariously

precaution

precawshun   precaution

precious

precipice

precise   precisely   precision

precocious

precorshun   precaution

predator

predict [predicting predicted]

predictable   prediction

preech   preach

preen [preening preened]

preest   priest

prefer [preferring preferred]

preferable   preferably

prefix   prefixes

pregnant   pregnancy

prehistoric

prejudice [prejudiced]

prekoshus   precocious

premature   prematurely

preoccupied

preparation   preparatory

prepare [preparing prepared]

preposition

prescribe [prescribed]

prescription

presence *[company]
   presents *[gifts]

presens   presence

present   presently
   [presenting presented]

presentation

preservation   preservative

preserve [preserving preserved]

preshure   pressure

preshus   precious

president   presidential

presise   precise

press [presses]
   [pressing pressed]

pressure   pressurised

presume [presumed]

presumably

pretect	protect
pretence	
pretend [pretending pretended]	
pretty prettier prettiest	
prevent prevention	
[preventing prevented]	
previde	provide
previous previously	
prey *[hunt-	pray *[to God]
[preying preyed]	
prezant	present
price *[cost]	prize *[award]
[pricing priced]	
priceless	
prick [pricking pricked]	
prickle [prickling prickled]	
prickly	
pride *[self-	pried *[snooped]
respect]	
pridict	predict

Check out **pre** as well

pridikshun	prediction
pries *[snoops]	prize *[award]
priest priestess	
prifer	prefer
prihistoric	prehistoric

prik	prick
prikul	prickle
prim primly primness	
primary	
prime [primed]	
prime minister	
prime number	
primitive	
primrose	
prince princely princess	
principal *[chief]	
principle *[rule, idea]	
prinse	prince
print [printing printed]	
priority priorities	
pripair	prepare
priscribe	prescribe
priscripshun	prescription
priservativ	preservative
prism	
prison prisoner	
prisume	presume
prisurve	preserve
pritend	pretend
prity	pretty
privacy	
private privately	
privent	prevent

privilege [privileged]

privvasee   privacy

prize *[award]   price *[cost]

probable   probably

probe [probing probed]

probible   probable

problem

proceed [proceeding proceeded]

process [processes]

  [processing processed]

procession

proclaim [proclaiming proclaimed]

prod   [prodding prodded]

produce [producing produced]

producer

product   production

produse   produce

profesee   prophecy

profeshun   profession

profession   professional

professor

profet   prophet *[seer]

                profit *[gain]

proffesor   professor

profile

profit *[gain]   prophet *[seer]

  [profiting profited]

progect   project

program *[computer]

  [programming programmed]

programme *[events]

progress [progressing progressed]

project   projector

promise [promising promised]

promiss   promise

promoshun   promotion

promote [promoted]

promotion   promotional

prompt [prompting prompted]

promptly

promt   prompt

prone

prong

pronoun

pronounce

  [pronouncing pronounced]

pronounciation pronunciation

pronown   pronoun

pronunciation

proof *[fact]   prove *[show]

proon   prune

proov   prove

prop [propping propped]

propel [propelled] propeller

proper   properly

property   properties

prophecy *[prediction]

prophesy *[predict]

[prophesies prophesied]

prophet prophetic

proporshun proportion

proportion

propose proposal

[proposing proposed]

prorn prawn

prose

prosecute [prosecuted]

proseed proceed

prosequte prosecute

prosess process

prospect

protecshun protection

protect protection

[protecting protected]

protective protectively

proteen protein

protein

protest [protesting protested]

proud prouder proudest

proudly

prove *[show] proof *[fact]

proverb proverbial

provide [providing provided]

provision provisional

provocative

provoke [provoked]

prow

prowd proud

prowl [prowling prowled]

pruf proof *[fact]

prove *[show]

prune [pruning pruned]

pruve prove

pry [pries prying pried]

pryde pride

psychological

psychology psychologist

pterodactyl

pub

puberty

public publicity

publication

publik public

publish publisher

[publishing published]

publisity publicity

puce

pudding

puddle

pudel puddle

puff [puffing puffed]

puffin

pule · pull

pull *[move] · pool *[water]
  [pulling pulled]

pullover

pulp [pulped]

pulpit

pulse

puma   pumas

pumel · pummel

pumkin · pumpkin

pump [pumping pumped]

pumpkin

pun

puncchual · punctual

punch [punches punching punched]

punctual   punctuality

punctuate   punctuation

puncture

punish [punishes]
  [punishing punished]

punishment

punkture · puncture

punnet

puny   punier   puniest

pupa   pupae

pupil

puppet

puppy   puppies

pur · per *[rate]

Check out **per** as well

purcentage · percentage

purchase [purchased]

purcushon · percussion

purd · purred

pure *[perfect] · purr *[cat]

pure   purely

purfict · perfect

purform · perform

purfume · perfume

purhaps · perhaps

purify [purified]

purm · perm

purmanent · permanent

puroved · proved

purple

purpose   purposely

purr *[cat] · per *[rate]
  [purring purred]

purrfikt · perfect

purse

pursecutid · persecuted

pursevure · persevere

pursue [pursuing pursued]

pursuit

push [pushes pushing pushed]

put *[place] [putting put]

putt *[golf] [putting putted]

putty

puzzle [puzzling puzzled]

pyjamas

pyle   pile

Check out
pi as well

pylon

pynt   pint

pyramid

pyrit   pirate

Pysees   Pisces

python

pyur   pure

qake — quake

qarrel — quarrel

qarter — quarter

qeschun — question

quack [quacking quacked]

quadratic equation

quadrilateral

quadruple [quadrupled]

quaint quainter quaintest

quak — quack

quake [quaking quaked]

Quaker

qualification

qualify [qualifies]
 [qualifying qualified]

quality qualities

quantity quantities

quarantine

quarrel quarrelsome
 [quarrelling quarrelled]

quarry quarries

quart

quarter

quartet

quarts *[measure]*

quartz *[mineral]*

quaree — quarry

quay *[sea]* — key *[lock, main]*

que — cue *[billiards]*
  — queue *[line up]*

queasy queasier queasiest

queen

queer queerer queerest

queerly

queery — query

queezy — queasy

queiten — quieten

quell [quelling quelled]

quench [quenching quenched]

query queries [querying queried]

quest

question [questioning questioned]

questionable

questionnaire

queue *[line]* cue *[ball]*
 [queueing queued]

quiat — quiet

quibble [quibbling quibbled]

quick quicker quickest

quicken [quickening quickened]

quickly quickness

quicksand

quick-tempered

quick-witted

quicley — quickly

quid

171

quier   **queer**

quiet *[silent]*   **quite** *[rather]*

quieten [quietening quietened]

quieter   quietest

quietly

quilt [quilted]

quirky   quirkier

quit *[leave, stop]*

    [quitting quitted quit]

quite *[rather]*   quiet *[silent]*

quitter

quiver [quivering quivered]

quiz   quizzes [quizzing quizzed]

quodratic   **quadratic**

Check out
qua as well

quolify   **qualify**

quolity   **quality**

quontity   **quantity**

quorrel   **quarrel**

quorry   **quarry**

quorter   **quarter**

quorts   **quarts**

             [measure]

             quartz

             [mineral]

quoruntine   **quarantine**

quota

quotashun   **quotation**

quotation

quote [quoting quoted]

qwack   **quack**

qwench   **quench**

qwick   **quick**

qwit   **quit**

qwod   **quad**

qworter   **quarter**

qwote   **quote**

rabbit

rabeys   rabies

rabies   rabid

race *[win]   raise *[lift]
   [racing raced]

racehorse

racial   racism   racist

rack *[shelf]   rake *[leaves]

racket *[din]   racquet *[bat]

radar

radiator

radio   radios

radioactive   radioactivity

radius

radyo   radio

raffle [raffling raffled]

raft [rafting rafted]

rag *[cloth]   rage *[fury]

rage *[fury] [raging raged]

ragged *[torn]   raged *[fury]

raid [raiding raided]

rail   railway

rain *[water]   reign *[rule]
   [raining rained]   rein *[horse]

rain ~coat ~drop

rain ~fall ~forest

raindeer   reindeer

rainy   rainier   rainiest

raise *[lift]   rays *[light]
   [raising raised]

raisin

raje   rage

rake

ram

ramble   rambler
   [rambling rambled]

rampage [rampaged]

ramparts

ramshackled

ran

ranch   ranches

rane   rain *[water]
            reign *[rule]
            rein *[horse]

rang

range [ranging ranged]

rank   rankings

ransack [ransacking ransacked]

ransom [ransomed]

rant [ranting ranted]

rap *[knock]   wrap *[pack]
   [rapping rapped]

rapper *[pop]   wrapper *[case]

rapid   rapidly

rare   rarer   rarest   rarely

rasberry   raspberry

rascal

rash   rashly   rashness

rashio   ratio

rashun   ration

rasisum   racism

raspberry   raspberries

rat [ratted]

rate [rating rated]

rather

rattle [rattling rattled]

ratty   rattier

ravenous   ravenously

ravioli

raw *[uncooked]*   roar *[lion]*

raydar   radar

rayl   rail

rayn   rain *[water]*

              reign *[rule]*

              rein *[horse]*

rays *[light]*   raise *[lift]*

rayser   razor

rayshal   racial

razor

reach [reaching reached]

react [reacting reacted]

reaction

read *[book]*   reed *[plant]*

  [reading read]

reader

ready   readier   readiest

real *[actual]*   reel *[spin]*

realise   realisation

  [realising realised]

realism   realist

realistic   realistically

reality

really *[truly]*   rely *[trust]*

reap   reaper [reaping reaped]

reappear   reappearance

  [reappearing reappeared]

rear *[horse]*   rare *[scarce]*

  [rearing reared]

rearrange [rearranged]

reason [reasoned]

reasonable   reasonably

reassure   reassurance

  [reassuring reassured]

rebal   rebel

rebel   rebellion

  [rebelling rebelled]

rebellious   rebelliously

rebild   rebuild

rebuild [rebuilding rebuilt]

rebuke [rebuked]

recall [recalling recalled]

recede [receding receded]

receipt

receive receiver

  [receiving received]

recent *[latest] resent *[grudge]

recently

reception receptionist

receptive

rech reach *[get]

  retch *[vomit]

  wretch *[person]

recipe recipes

recite recital [reciting recited]

reckless recklessly

recklessness

reckon [reckoning reckoned]

reclaim [reclaiming reclaimed]

recline [reclining reclined]

recognise recognisable

  [recognising recognised]

recognition

recoil [recoiling recoiled]

recollect recollection

  [recollecting recollected]

recommend recommendation

  [recommending recommended]

reconcile [reconciled]

reconciliation

reconnect [reconnected]

reconsider

  [reconsidering reconsidered]

reconsile reconcile

reconstruct [reconstructed]

record [recording recorded]

recover recoverable

  [recovering recovered]

recovery recoveries

recreation recreational

recruit recruitment

  [recruiting recruited]

rectangle rectangular

recur [recurring recurred]

recurrence recurrent

recycle [recycled]

red *[colour] read *[book]

redden [reddening]

reddy ready

redial [redialling redialled]

redo [redoing redone]

redouble [redoubled]

reduce reduction

  [reducing reduced]

redundancy redundant

reduse reduce

reech reach

reed *[plant] read *[book]

reek *[smell] wreak *[havoc]

175

reel *[spin]   real *[true]

reeson   reason

refer [referring referred]

referee [refereeing refereed]

reference [referenced]

refill   refillable [refilling refilled]

refine [refined]   refinement

reflect   reflective

[reflecting reflected]

reflection

reflex   reflexes

refrain [refrained]

refresh   refreshment

[refreshing refreshed]

refrigerate [refrigerated]

refrigeration   refrigerator

refuel [refuelling refuelled]

refuge *[shelter]

refugee *[flee]   refugees

refund [refunding refunded]

refuree   referee

refuse   refusal [refusing refused]

regain [regaining regained]

regard   regardless

[regarding regarded]

regatta   regattas

regay   reggae

regect   reject

reggae

regiment   regimental

region   regional

register   registration

[registering registered]

regler   regular

regret [regretting regretted]

regretful   regretfully

regrettable   regrettably

regular   regularly   regularity

rehearse   rehearsal

[rehearsing rehearsed]

reheat [reheating reheated]

reign *[rule]   rain *[water]

rein *[horse]

[reigning reigned]

rein *[horse]   rain *[water]

reign *[rule]

reindeer

reinforce   reinforcement

[reinforcing reinforced]

reject [rejecting rejected]

rejection

rejiment   regiment

rejister   register

rejoice [rejoicing rejoiced]

rejuce   reduce

rejun   region

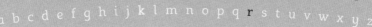

rekollekt   recollect

rekommend   recommend

rekord   record

rekwest   request

relate [relating related]

relation   relationship

relative   relatively

relavent   relevant

relax   relaxation

  [relaxes relaxing relaxed]

relay [relaying relayed]

release [releasing released]

relegate   relegation

  [relegating relegated]

relent [relenting relented]

relentless   relentlessly

relevance   relevant

reliable   reliably

relief

relieve [relieved]

religion

religious   religiously

relijion   religion

relly   really

reluctance

reluctant   reluctantly

rely *[trust]   really *[truly]

  [relies relying relied]

remain   remainder

  [remaining remained]

remark   remarkable

  [remarking remarked]

rember   remember

remember

  [remembering remembered]

remind   reminder

  [reminding reminded]

remote   remoter

remotely   remoteness

remove   removal

  [removing removed]

rendezvous

renew [renewing renewed]

renewable

repair [repairing repaired]

repay   repayment

  [repaying repaid]

repayd   repaid

repeat [repeating repeated]

repeatedly

repel [repelled]   repellent

repent [repenting repented]

repere   repair

repete   repeat

repetition   repetitious

repetitive   repetitively

replace   replaceable
[replacing replaced]

replacement

replay [replaying replayed]

reply   replies [replying replied]

report   reportedly   reporter
[reporting reported]

represent   representation
[representing represented]

representative

reprimand [reprimanded]

reproduce
[reproducing reproduced]

reproduction   reproductive

reptile   reptilian

repulsive   repulsively

reputation

request [requesting requested]

require   requirement
[requiring required]

rere   rare *[scarce]

               rear *[back,
                      horse]

rerite   rewrite

rerote   rewrote

resalootion   resolution

rescue   rescuer
[rescuing rescued]

research [researches]
[researching researched]

resseet   receipt

reseeve   receive

resemble [resembling resembled]

resemblance

resent *[grudge]   recent *[latest]

resentful   resentment

resepshun   reception

reservation

reserve [reserved]

reservoir

residence   resident

residenchal   residential

residential

resign   resignation
[resigning resigned]

resipy   recipe

resist [resisting resisted]

resistance   resistant

resite   recite

reskue   rescue

resle   wrestle

resolution

resolve [resolving resolved]

resons   reasons

resort [resorting resorted]

resource   resourceful

respect   respectable
   [respecting respected]
respectful   respectfully
respond [responded]
response   responsibility
responsibilities
responsible   responsibly
resstront   restaurant
rest [resting rested]
restaurant
restful   restfully
restless   restlessly
restore   restoration
   [restoring restored]
restrain   restraint
   [restraining restrained]
restrict   restriction
   [restricting restricted]
result [resulting resulted]
resurvwa   reservoir
resuscitate [resuscitated]
resuscitation
resycle   recycle
retain [retaining retained]
retaliate [retaliated]
retch *[vomit] [retching]
   wretch *[person]
rethink [rethinking rethought]

retire   retirement
   [retiring retired]
retort [retorting retorted]
retrace [retracing retraced]
retreat [retreating retreated]
retrieve   retrievable
   [retrieving retrieved]
retriever
retrospect   retrospective
return [returning returned]
reunion
reunite [reuniting reunited]
reveal [revealing revealed]
revenge   revengeful
reverse   reversible
   [reversing reversed]
review [reviewed]
revise [revising revised]
revision
revive [reviving revived]
revolt [revolting revolted]
revolution   revolutionary
revolutionise [revolutionised]
revolve [revolving revolved]
revolver
reward [rewarding rewarded]
rewind [rewinding rewound]
rezzavwa   reservoir

rfter	after
rfternon	afternoon
rheumatism	
rhino rhinoceros	
rhomboid rhombus	
rhubarb	
rhyme [rhyming rhymed]	
rhythm rhythmical	
riacshun	reaction
riact	react
riality	reality
rib	
ribbon	
ribellius	rebellious
rice *[food]	rise *[up]
riceipt	receipt
rich richly richness	
Richter Scale [the]	
rickety	
riclaim	reclaim
ricoil	recoil
rid riddance	
riddle	
ride rider [riding rode ridden]	
ridge ridged	
ridiculous ridiculously	
rifle [rifling rifled]	
riflect	reflect

right *[correct]	write *[pen]
right rightly rightful	
right-handed	
rigid rigidly	
rim *[edge]	rhyme *[poetry]
rimless rimmed	
rimain	remain

Check out
re as well

rimark	remark
rimember	remember
rimote	remote
rimoval	removal
rind	
ring *[circle]	wring *[wet]
ring *[bell] [ringing rang rung]	
rink	
rinkle	wrinkle
rino	rhino
rinse [rinsing rinsed]	
riot [rioting rioted]	
riotous riotously	
rip *[tear] [ripping ripped]	ripe *[ready]
ripair	repair
ripe ripeness	
ripeat	repeat

ripen [ripening ripened]

riply	reply
riport	report

ripple [rippling rippled]

ripulsiv	repulsive
riquest	request
riquire	require
rise *[up]	rice *[food]

[rises rising risen]

riserve	reserve
risine	resign
risist	resist

risk [risking risked]

risky   riskier   riskiest

risolve	resolve
risort	resort

risotto

risource	resource
rispect	respect
rispectabul	respectable
risponsibul	responsible
ritch	rich
rithum	rhythm

ritual

riturn	return

rival   rivalry

rivenge	revenge

river   riverside

rivet [riveting riveted]

ro	roe *[deer]
	row *[boat]
road *[street]	rode *[bike]
	rowed *[boat]

roam *[wander]   Rome *[city]
[roaming roamed]

roar *[lion]   raw *[uncooked]
[roaring roared]

roast [roasting roasted]

rob [robbed]   robbery

robe [robed]

robin

robot   robotic

rock [rocking rocked]

rocket

rocky   rockier   rockiest

rod *[fishing]	rode *[bike]
	road *[street]
	rowed *[boat]

rodent

roial	royal
rok	rock
roket	rocket

role *[actor]

roll *[move] [rolling rolled]   roller

Roman   Roman Catholic

romance

romanse   romance
romantic   romantically
rombus   rhombus
Romen   Roman
rondayvoo   rendezvous
rong   wrong
roobarb   rhubarb
roof   roofless
rook   rookery
room   roomful   roomy
roomer   rumour
roost [roosting roosted]
rooster
root *[plant]   route *[way]
   [rooting rooted]
rooteen   routine
rope [roped]
rore   roar *[lion]
           raw *[fresh]
rose *[flower]   rows *[boat]
rosette
rost   roast
rosy
rot [rotting rotted]
rota *[list]   rotor *[blade]
rotashun   rotation
rotate [rotating rotated]
rotation

rote *[repeat]   wrote *[pen]
rotor *[blade]   rota *[list]
rotten
rough   rougher   roughly
round   rounder   roundly
roundabout
rounders
route *[way]   root *[plant]
routine
row *[boat] [rowing rowed]
row *[noise] [rowed]   rowdy
rownd   round
rows *[boat]   rose *[flower]
royal   royally   royalty
rub [rubbing rubbed]
rubarb   rhubarb
rubber   rubbery
rubbish [rubbished]   rubbishy
rubble
ruby   rubies
rucksack
rudder
rude   ruder   rudest
rude   rudely   rudeness
ruel   rule
Rugby League   Rugby Union
rugged
ruin [ruining ruined]

rule ruler [ruling ruled]

rumatic   rheumatic

rumatisum   rheumatism

rumble [rumbling rumbled]

rumour [rumoured]

rumple [rumpled]

run [running ran] runner

rung *[ring]   wrung *[wet]

runny runnier runniest

runway

rush [rushing rushed]

Rushun   Russian

russel   rustle

rust rusted rusty

rustle rustler

 [rustling rustled]

rut [rutted]

rute   root *[plant]

         route *[way]

ruthless ruthlessly

ruthlessness

ryce   rice

ryme   rhyme

ryval   rival

sabbath

sachel   satchel

sack [sacking sacked]

sacrifice   sacrificial
   [sacrificing sacrificed]

sad   sadder   sadly   sadness

sadden [saddening saddened]

saddle [saddling saddled]

safari   safaris

safe   safer   safely

safety

saffire   sapphire

saftey   safety

sag [sagging sagged]   saggy

said

saif   safe

sail *[boat]   sale *[goods]
   [sailing sailed]

sailor

saim   same

saint   saintly

saiv   save

sak   sack *[bag,
                    destroy]
             sake *[sake of]

sake

sakrifise   sacrifice

salad

salary   salaries

sale *[goods]   sail *[boat]

salery   salary

sales   ~man ~person ~woman

saliva

salmon

salon

salt   salty   saltier

salute [saluting saluted]

salvage   [salvaged]

salvige   salvage

Samaritan

same   sameness

samon   salmon

sample [sampling sampled]

sand [sanding sanded]

sandbank   sandpit

sandwich   sandwiches

sandy   sandier   sandiest

sane   sanely   saner

sanity

sank

Santa Claus

sanwich   sandwich

sapphire

sarcastic   sarcastically

sardine

sari

sarkastik	sarcastic
sarm	psalm
sat	
Satan Satanic	
satchel	
satellite	
Saterday	Saturday
satisfactory	
satisfy satisfaction	
[satisfying satisfied]	
Saturday	
sauce *[dip]	source *[start]
saucepan	
saucer	
sauna	
saunter [sauntering sauntered]	
sausage	
sause	sauce *[liquid]
	source *[origin]
savage savagely	
[savaging savaged]	
save [saving saved] saver	
savige	savage
saviour	
saw *[see]	soar *[fly]
	sore *[hurt]
saw *[cut] [sawn] sawdust	
saxophone saxophonist	

say [saying said]	
saym	same
saynt	saint
sayvyer	saviour
scab scabby scabbier	
scaffold scaffolding	
scair	scare
scald [scalding scalded]	
scale [scaling scaled]	
scalp [scalped]	
scalpel	
scaly scalier scaliest	
scam	
scamper [scampered]	
scampi	
scan [scanning scanned]	
scandal scandalous	
scanner	
scar *[mark] scare *[shock]	
scarce scarcely scarcity	
scare *[shock] scar *[mark]	
scarecrow	
scarf scarves	
scarlet	
scarse	scarce
scary scarier scariest	
scate	skate
scatter [scattering scattered]	

scatty   scattier   scattiest

scavenge   scavenger

 [scavenging scavenged]

scaw   score

scene *[stage]   seen *[eyes]

scenery

scent *[smell]   sent *[gone]

                        cent *[money]

scerd   scared

scery   scary

schedule [scheduled]

scholar   scholarship

school   ~boy ~child ~girl

science   scientist

scientific   scientifically

scill   skill

scin   skin

scip   skip

scissors

scoff [scoffing scoffed]

scolar   scholar

scold *[tell off]   scald *[burn]

scone

scool   school

scoop [scooped]

scoot   scooter

scorch [scorching scorched]

score [scored]   scoreboard

scorpion

Scot   Scotch   Scottish

scout [scouted]

scowl [scowling scowled]

scrabble [scrabbled]

scrach   scratch

scramble [scrambled]

scrap *[junk] [scrapped]

scrape *[remove]

scratch [scratches]

 [scratching scratched]

scratchy   scratchier

scrawl [scrawled]

scrawny   scrawnier

screach   screech

scream

screech   screeches

 [screeching screeched]

screen   screenwriter

screme   scream

screw [screwed] screwdriver

screwpel   scruple

scribble   scribbler

 [scribbling scribbled]

scribe

scripcher   scripture

script   scriptwriter

scripture

scroll [scrolled]

scroo   screw

scrooge

scrornee   scrawny

scrounge   scrounger

scrownge   scrounge

scrub [scrubbing scrubbed]

scruff   scruffy   scruffier

scrum

scrunch [scrunches]
  [scrunching scrunched]

scuba

scuff [scuffing scuffed]

scuffle [scuffling scuffled]

sculpcher   sculpture

sculpt [sculpted]

sculptor *[artist]

sculpture *[carving]

scum   scummy

scurry [scurrying scurried]

scuttle [scuttled]

scwelchey   squelchy

sea *[waves]   see *[eyes]

sea-anenome

sea   ~front ~gull ~horse

sea   ~shore ~sick ~side

sead   said *[say]

      seed *[plant]

seak   seek *[look for]

      Sikh *[religion]

seal [sealing sealed]

Check out
ce as well

sealing   ceiling *[roof]
   *[fastening]

seam *[cloth]   seem *[appear]

sean   scene *[stage]

      seen *[eyes]

search [searches searched]

searching   searchlight

seasaw   seesaw

sease   cease *[stop]

      seize *[grab]

season   seasonal

seat [seating seated]

secendry   secondary

second   secondly

secondary

secrecy

secretary   secretaries

secure [secured]   securely

security

sed   said

see *[eyes]   sea *[waves]

  [seeing saw seen]

seekrit   secret

seed [seeded]   seedling

seel   seal

seeling   ceiling

seem *[appear]   seam *[cloth]
   [seeming seemed]

seen *[see]   scene *[stage]

seereez   series

seeriul   cereal

seesaw [seesawed]

seeson   season

seet   seat

seid   said

seize *[grab]   cease *[stop]

sekure   secure

sekwence   sequence

sekwin   sequin

seldom

selebrate   celebrate

select [selecting selected]

selection   selective

selery   celery

self   selves

selfish   selfishly

selfless   selflessly

sell *[shop]   cell *[prison]

seller *[sales   cellar *[room]
       person]

Sellotape™

Selsius   Celsius

selves

seme   seam *[cloth]
           seem *[appear]

sement   cement

semetery   cemetery

semi   ~circle ~circular

semi   ~colon ~conscious

semi-final

send [sending sent]   sender

sene   scene *[stage]
        seen *[eyes]

sensashunal   sensational

sensation   sensational

sense   senseless

sensible   sensibly

sensitive   sensitively

sensitivity   sensitivities

sent *[gone]   scent *[smell]

senta   centre

sentence

sentens   sentence

senter   centre

Check out
ce as well

sentigrade   centigrade

sentimental	sentimentality
sentimetre	centimetre
sentipede	centipede
sentral	central
sentry	sentries
sentury	century
separate	separately
separation	
sepret	separate
September	
sequence	sequential
sequin [sequinned]	
ser	sir
seramic	ceramic
serch	search
serchin	searching
sereal	cereal *[grain]
	serial
	*[sequence]
seremonee	ceremony
serf *[slave]	surf *[sea]
serface	surface
sergeant	
sergeon	surgeon
serial *[sequence]	cereal *[grain]
serialisation [serialising]	
series	
serious	seriously

sermon	
sername	surname
serpent	
serprise	surprise
sertain	certain
sertificate	certificate
servant	
serve [serving served]	
service [serviced]	
sesshun	session
session	
set *[put]	seat *[sitting]
	sett *[badger]
setentes	sentences
settee	
setting	
settle [settling settled]	
seveir	severe
seven	seventeen seventh
sevon	seven
seventy	seventieth
several	
severe	severely severity
sevnteen	seventeen
sevrel	several
sew *[clothes]	sow *[seed]
[sewing sewn]	so *[thus]
sewer	sewerage

sewn *[clothes]   sown *[seed]

sex

sey   say

sfere   sphere

shabby   shabbier

shack

shackle [shackled]

shade   shaded   shady

shadow   shadowy

shaft

shaggy   shaggier

shaid   shade

shaip   shape

shair   share

shake [shaking shaken]

shaky   shakier

shall

shallow   shallower

shamble   shambles

shame *[guilt]   sham *[fake]

shameful   shamefully

shameless   shamelessly

shampain   champagne

shampoo [shampooed]

shan't [shall not]

shape   shapeless   shapely

shark   shark-infested

sharp   sharply   sharpness

sharpen   sharpener
  [sharpening sharpened]

shatter [shattered]

shave [shaving shaved]

shaw   shore *[sea]

              sure *[certain]

shawl

shawt   short

she   she's [she is, has]

shear *[clip]   sheer *[steep]

shed *[hut, hair]

she'd *[she had, would]

shedule   schedule

sheep   sheepish   sheepishly

sheer *[steep]   shear *[clip]

sheet   sheeting

sheild   shield

shelf   shelves

shell [sea]   she'll *[she will]

shelter [sheltering sheltered]

shepherd

sheriff

shert   shirt

she's [she is, she has]

shi   she *[female]

              shy *[timid]

shield [shielding shielded]

shier   sheer

190

shiffon   chiffon

shift [shifting shifted]   shifty

shimmer   shimmery
   [shimmering shimmered]

shin *[leg]

shine *[sun] [shining shone]

shingle   shingly

shiny   shinier   shiniest

ship [shipping shipped]

shipwreck [shipwrecked]

shirk [shirking shirked]

shirt

shiver   shivery
   [shivering shivered]

sho   show

shoal

shoar   shore *[sea]
                     sure *[certain]

shock [shocking shocked]

shoddy   shoddier

shoe *[foot]   shoo *[away]
   [shoes shoing shoed]

shoe   ~horn ~lace

shofer   chauffeur

shok   shock

sholder   shoulder

shone *[lit up,   shown
        polished]   *[did show]

shoo *[away]   shoe *[foot]
   [shooes shooing shooed]

shood   should

shook

shool   school

shoot *[target]   chute *[slide]
   [shooting shot]

shoow   shoe

shop [shopping shopped]

shoplifter [shoplifting]

shore *[sea]   sure *[certain]

shorn

short   shortly   shortness

shortage

shorten [shortened]

shot

should

shouldent   shouldn't

shoulder

shouldn't [should not]

shout [shouting shouted]

shove [shoving shoved]

shovel [shovelling shovelled]

show [showing showed]

shower   showery

showt   shout

showy   showier   showiest

shrank

shred   shredder
[shredding shredded]

shreik   shriek

shrew   shrewish

shrewd   shrewdly

shrewdness

shriek [shrieking shrieked]

shrill   shrilly

shrimp [shrimping]

shrink [shrinking shrunk]

shrivel [shrivelled]

Shrove Tuesday

shrub   shrubbery

shrued   shrewd

shrug [shrugging shrugged]

shrunk   shrunken

shud   should

shudder [shuddering shuddered]

shudent   shouldn't
                [should not]

shuffle   shuffly
  [shuffling shuffled]

shun [shunned]

shunt [shunting shunted]

shut *[close]   chute *[slide]
  [shutting shut]

shuttle

shuv   shove

shuvel   shovel

shy *[timid]   shyly   shyness

shy *[horse] [shies shying shied]

si   sigh

siad   said

Siamese

sichuayshun   situation

sick *[ill]   Sikh *[religion]

sicken [sickening sickened]

side [siding sided]

side   ~burns ~ways

sider   cider

sidle [sidling sidled]

sied   sighed

siege

siense   science

sieve [sieved]

sift [sifting sifted]

sigaret   cigarette

sigh [sighing sighed]

sight *[see]   site *[place]

sightseeing   sightseer

sign   signpost

signachure   signature

signal [signalled]

signature

signet *[ring]   cygnet *[swan]

significant   significantly

sik	sick
Sikh *[religion]	seek *[look]
siksth	sixth
silee	silly
silence silencer	
[silencing silenced]	
silent silently	
silhouette	
silk silken silky	
sillabul	syllable
sillooet	silhouette
silly sillier silliest	
silver silvery	
simbol	cymbal *[music]
	symbol *[sign]
simese	Siamese
similar similarity	
simmer [simmering]	
simmetrical	symmetrical
simpathetic	sympathetic
simple simpler simplest	
simplicity simply	
simplify [simplifies]	
[simplifying simplified]	
simpul	simple
since *[from]	sins *[bad]
sincere sincerely sincerity	
sindrome	syndrome

sinema	cinema
sinful sinfully	
sing *[music] singer	
[singing sang]	
singe *[burn] [singeing singed]	
single singly	
sinister	
sink [sinking sank sunk]	
sinmer	cinema
sinner	
sinonim	synonym
sinse	since
sip [sipping sipped]	
sir	

Check out cir as well

sircul	circle
sircus	circus
siren	
siringe	syringe
sirrup	syrup
sise	size
sissors	scissors
sissy sissies	
sister sisterly	
sistes	sisters
sit [sitting sat]	

193

site *[place]   sight *[seeing]
siteseeing   sightseeing
sitizen   citizen
sitrus   citrus
situate [situated]
situation
sity   city
sityooashun   situation
sive   sieve
sivil   civil
sivilisashun   civilisation
six   sixth
sixteen   sixteenth
sixty   sixtieth
size   sizeable
sizzle [sizzling sizzled]
skab   scab
skaffold   scaffold
skale   scale
skalp   scalp
skaly   scaly
skate [skating skated]
skateboard   skateboarder
skeleton   skeletal
skert   skirt
sketch   sketches
  [sketching sketched]
sketchy   sketchier

skewer [skewered]
ski *[sport]   sky *[air]
  [skis skiing skied]
skid *[slip]   skied *[sport]
  [skidding skidded]
skilful   skilfully
skill [skilled]
skim [skimming skimmed]
skin [skinned]
skinny   skinnier   skinniest
skint
skip [skipping skipped]
skirt [skirting skirted]
skittle
skold   scald *[burn]
              scold *[tell off]
skon   scone
skool   school
skript   script
skufful   scuffle
skull
skuttling   scuttling
skwall   squall
skware   square
skwobble   squabble
skwod   squad
skwodron   squadron
skwonder   squander

skwosh	squash
skwot	squat
sky *[space]	ski *[sport]
sky ~scraper ~wards	
slab	
slack slacker slackest	
slaiv	slave
slam [slamming slammed]	
slander slanderous	
slang slanging match	
slant [slanting slanted]	
slap [slapping slapped]	
slash [slashing slashed]	
slate	
slaughter [slaughtered]	
slave slavery	
slay [slaying slew slain]	
sleap	sleep
sleat	sleet
sleave	sleeve
sledge sledging	
sleek sleekly sleekness	
sleep [sleeping slept]	
sleepless sleeplessness	
sleepy sleepier sleepiest	
sleet sleeting	
sleeve sleeveless	
slege	sledge

sleigh *[snow] slay *[kill]	
slender slenderness	
slep	sleep
slepin	sleeping
slept	
sley	slay *[kill]
	sleigh *[snow]
slice [slicing sliced]	
slick slickly slickness	
slide [sliding slid]	
slied	slide
slight slightly	
slik	slick
slim *[thin]	
slime *[gooey] slimy	
sling [slinging slung]	
slip [slipping slipped]	
slipper	
slippery slippy slippier	
slise	slice
slit slitty	
slither [slithered] slithery	
slobber slobbery	
[slobbering slobbered]	
slog [slogging slogged]	
slooth	sleuth
slope [sloping sloped]	
slorter	slaughter

slot [slotting slotted]

slouch [slouching slouched]

slow slower slowly

sludge sludgy

slug sluggish sluggishly

slum slummy

slumber [slumbering slumbered]

slump [slumped]

slung

slurp [slurping slurped]

slush slushy

sly slyly slyness

slymee slimy

smack [smacking smacked]

small smaller smallest

smart smarter smartest

smartly smartness

smash [smashing smashed]

smear [smearing smeared]

smell [smelling smelt]

smelly smellier smelliest

smile [smiling smiled]

smiley smilier smiliest

smithereens

smog smoggy

smoke [smoking smoked]

smoky smokier smokiest

smooth [smoothing smoothed]

smoothie

smoothly smoothness

smother [smothering smothered]

smoulder

[smouldering smouldered]

smudge smudged smudgy

smug smugly smugness

smuggle smuggler

[smuggling smuggled]

smyle smile

snack [snacking snacked]

snaik snake

snail

snair snare

snak snack

snake [snaking] snakey

snale snail

snap [snapping snapped]

snare [snaring snared]

snarl [snarling snarled]

snatch [snatches]

[snatching snatched]

sneaky sneakier sneakiest

sneer [sneering sneered]

sneeze [sneezing sneezed]

snifel sniffle

sniff [sniffing sniffed]

sniffle [sniffling sniffled]

snigger [sniggering sniggered]

snip [snipped]

sniper

snivel [snivelling snivelled]

sno   snow

snob   snobbery

snooker [snookered]

snoop [snooping snooped]

snooty

snooze [snoozing snoozed]

snorcul   snorkel

snore [snoring snored]

snorkel [snorkelling]

snort [snorting snorted]

snout

snow [snowing snowed]

snow   ~ball ~boarding ~bound

snow   ~drift ~drop ~fall

snow   ~flake ~man ~plough

snow   ~shoes ~storm

snowt   snout

snowy   snowier   snowiest

snub [snubbing snubbed]

snuff [snuffed]

snuffle [snuffling snuffled]

snuffly

snug   snuggle   snuggly
  [snuggling snuggled]

snuze   snooze

so *[thus]   sew *[clothes]
           sow *[seeds]

soak [soaking soaked]

soal   sole *[one]
       soul *[spirit]

soap   soapy   soapier

soar *[fly]   saw *[see, cut]
         sore *[hurt]

sob [sobbing sobbed]

soccer

social   sociable   socially

sock

socker   soccer

socket

soda

sodden

sofa

soffen   soften

soft   softly   softness

soften [softened]

software

soggy   soggier   soggiest

soil [soiling soiled]

sok   sock *[foot]
       soak *[water]

solar

sold

solder *[metal] [soldering]

soldier *[army] [soldiering]

sole *[one]   soul *[spirit]

solejur   soldier

solem   solemn

solemn   solemnly

soler   solar

solger   soldier

solicitor

solid   solidly

solitary

solo   soloist

solt   salt

solution

solve [solving solved]

som   some

some *[amount]   sum *[add]

some   ~body ~how ~one ~thing

some   ~times ~what ~where

somersault [somersaulted]

son *[boy]   sun *[shine]

song

sonic

soon   sooner   soonest

soop   soup

soor   saw

soot *[coal]   suit *[clothes]

soothe [soothing soothed]

sooty   sootier   sootiest

sopey   soapy

sopping

soppy   soppier   soppiest

sor   sore

sorce   sauce *[liquid]

        source *[origin]

sorcer   saucer

sorcerer   sorceress   sorcery

sord   sword

sordust   sawdust

sore *[hurt]   saw *[see, cut]

        soar *[fly]

sorely

sorn   sawn

sorna   sauna

soro   sorrow

sorrow   sorrowful

sorrowfully

sorry   sorrier   sorriest

sorserer   sorcerer

sort *[kind]   sought *[seek]

sory   sorry

soshabul   sociable

soshall   social

sosiety   society

sossige   sausage

sought *[seek]   sort *[kind]

soul *[spirit]   sole *[one]

sound   soundly
  [sounding sounded]

soundless   soundlessly

soup

sour   sourly   sourness

source *[start]   sauce *[dip]

south   southern   southerner

souvenir

sovereign

sovren   sovereign

sow *[seed]   sew *[clothes]

sow *[pig]   so *[thus]

sown *[seed]   sewn *[clothes]

sownd   sound

sowr   sour

sowth   south

space [spacing spaced]

space   ~man ~ship ~suit

spade

spagety   spaghetti

spaghetti

spair   spare

spam

span [spanning spanned]

spaner   spanner

spangle [spangled]

spaniel

spank [spanking spanked]

spanner

spanyel   spaniel

spare [sparing spared]

spark [sparking sparked]

sparkeling   sparkling

sparkle   sparkly
  [sparkling sparkled]

sparrow   sparrowhawk

spase   space

spatter [spattering spattered]

speach   speech

speak [speaking spoke]

spear   spearmint

special   specially

species

speckle   speckled

spectacles   spectacled

spectacular   spectacularly

spectator

speech   speechless

speed [speeding sped]

speedometer

speedy   speedier   speediest

speek   speak

speer   spear

speesheez   species

spektakular   spectacular

199

spell [spelling spelt]

spellbinding   spellbound

spend [spending spent]

spensiv   expensive

speshul   special

sphere   spherical

spice   spiced   spicy

spider   spidery

spied

spike [spiking spiked]

spikey   spikier   spikiest

spill [spilling spilt]

spin *[turn]   spine *[back]

[spinning spun]

spinach

spine *[back]   spin *[turn]

spineless   spinelessly

spinich   spinach

spining   spinning

spiral

spire

spise   spice

spit *[saliva] [spitting spat]

spite *[nasty]

spiteful   spitefully

splash [splashing splashed]

splashy   splashier

splatter [splattered]

splender   splendour

splendid   splendidly

splendour

splinter [splintered]

split [splitting]

splodge   splodgy

splutter [spluttering spluttered]

spoak   spoke

spoil [spoiling spoilt]

spoiler

spoke   spoken   spokesman

sponge [sponging sponged]

spongy   spongier   spongiest

spook [spooked]

spooky   spookier   spookiest

spoon [spooning spooned]

spoonful

sport [sporting sported]

sporty   sportier   sportiest

sportsman   sportswoman

spot [spotting spotted]

spotless   spotlessly

spotlight [spotlit]

spotty   spottier   spottiest

spout [spouting spouted]

sprain

sprang

sprawl [sprawled]

spray [spraying sprayed]

spread [spreading spread]

spred   spread

spring [springing sprang sprung]

spring   springtime

springy   springier

sprinkle   sprinkler
  [sprinkling sprinkled]

sprint [sprinting sprinted]

sprinter

spritely

sprout [sprouting sprouted]

sprung

spruys   surprise

spuk   spook

spur [spurred]

spurt [spurting spurted]

sputter [sputtering sputtered]

spy [spies spying spied]

spyke   spike

spyne   spine

spyral   spiral

spyre   spire

squabble [squabbling squabbled]

squad   squadron

squall   squally   squallier

squander
  [squandering squandered]

square   squarely

squash [squashing squashed]

squashy   squashier

squat [squatting squatted]

squawk [squawking squawked]

squeak [squeaking squeaked]

squeaky

squeakier   squeakiest

squeal [squealing squealed]

squeek   squeak

squeeze [squeezing squeezed]

squelch   squelchy
  [squelching squelched]

squerm   squirm

squert   squirt

squid

squiggle   squiggly

squint [squinting squinted]

squirel   squirrel

squirm [squirming squirmed]

squirrel

squirt [squirting squirted]

squish [squished]   squishy

squork   squawk

stab [stabbing stabbed]

stabel   stable

stabilisers

stable

stachue   statue

stack [stacking stacked]

stadium

staek   stake *[post]

            steak *[beef]

staer   stair *[step]

            stare *[gaze]

staff [staffing staffed]

stag *[deer]

stage *[time, theatre]

stagger [staggering staggered]

stagnant

stail   stale

stain [staining stained]

stair *[step]   stare *[gaze]

stait   state

stak   stack

stake *[post]   steak *[beef]

stalactite *[down]

stalagmite *[up]

stale   stalemate

stalegmite   stalagmite *[up]

stalektite   stalactite

            *[down]

stalk *[follow]   stork *[bird]

  [stalking stalked]

stalker

stall [stalling stalled]

stallion

stalyen   stallion

stamp [stamping stamped]

stampede [stampeding]

stand [standing stood]

stand-offish

stane   stain

stank

stapel   staple

staple [stapled]   stapler

star *[sky]   stare *[gaze]

starboard

stare *[gaze]   stair *[step]

staree   starry

starlight   starlit

starling

starred   starry   starrier

start [starting started]

startle [startling startled]

starve   starvation

  [starving starved]

stash [stashed]

stashun   station

state [stating stated]

statement   statesman

station   stationmaster

stationary *[still]

stationery *[paper]

statue

stay [staying stayed]

stayje   stage

steady   steadier   steadiest

steak *[beef]   stake *[post]

steal *[take]   steel *[iron]

   [stealing stole stolen]

stealth   stealthy

steam [steaming steamed]

steamy   steamier   steamiest

stedy   steady

steel *[iron]   steal *[take]

steep   steeply   steepness

steeple   ~chase   ~jack

steer [steering steered]

stencil   stencilling

stensil   stencil

step [stepping stepped]

ster   stir

stern   sternly   sternness

stew [stewing stewed]

steward   stewardess

stewdent   student

stich   stitch

stick [sticking stuck]

sticker

sticky   stickier   stickiest

stier   steer

stiff   stiffer   stiffest

stiffen [stiffened]

stiffly   stiffness

stik   stick

stiky   sticky

stile *[step]   style *[type]

still   stiller   stillness

stilts

sting [stinging stung]

stingy   stingier   stingiest

stink [stinking stank stunk]

stir [stirring stirred]

stirrup

stitch   stitches

   [stitching stitched]

stoal   stole

stoan   stone

stoat

stocking

stodge   stodgy   stodgier

stole   stolen

stomach   stomach-ache

stomp [stomping stomped]

stone   Stone Age

stony   stonier   stoniest

stood

stool

stoop [stooping stooped]

stop [stopping stopped]

stopper

stopt   stopped

store [storing stored]

storey *[floor]   story *[tale]

stork *[bird]   stalk *[follow]

storm   stormy   stormier

story *[tale]   storey *[floor]

storyteller   storytelling

stout   stouter   stoutest

stoutly   stoutness

stove

stowt   stout

straey   stray

straggle   straggly
   [straggling straggled]

straight   straighter

straightforward

straighten   straightened

strain [straining strained]

strand   stranded

strane   strain

strange   strangely

stranger

strangle   strangler
   [strangling strangled]

straw

strawberry   strawberries

stray [straying strayed]

strayt   straight

streak   streaky   streakier
   [streaking streaked]

stream   streamer
   [streaming streamed]

strech   stretch

streem   stream

street   streetwise

strength

strengthen [strengthened]

strenth   strength

stress   stressed   stressful

stressfully

stretch   stretches
   [stretching stretched]

stretcher

strict   stricter   strictest

strictly   strictness

stride [striding strode]

strike [striking struck]

strikt   strict

string   stringing   stringy

stripe   striped   stripey

stroad   strode

strobrey   strawberry

strode

stroke [stroking stroked]

stroll [strolling strolled]

strong   stronger   strongly

strop   stroppy   stroppier

stror   straw

strorbury   strawberry

struck

struggle [struggling struggled]

strung

stryke   strike

stub [stubbed]

stubble   stubbly

stubborn   stubbornly

stubbornness

stubel   stubble

stuck   stuck-up

student

studio

study   studies [studying studied]

studyo   studio

stue   stew

stuff [stuffing stuffed]

stuffy   stuffier   stuffiest

stule   stool

stumack   stomach

stumble   stumbled

stumok   stomach

stun [stunning stunned]

stung

stunk

stupendous

stunt   stuntman

stupid   stupider   stupidest

stupidly   stupidity

stur   stir

sturn   stern

stutter   stutterer
 [stuttering stuttered]

sty   sties

style *[type]   stile *[step]

subdued

suberb   suburb *[town]
            superb *[great]

subject

submarine   submariner

submerge [submerged]

submurje   submerge

subset

substance

substantial   substantially

substence   substance

substitute   substitution
 [substituting substituted]

subtract   subtraction
 [subtracting subtracted]

suburb   suburban   suburbia

subzero

205

succeed [succeeding succeeded]

success   successes

successful   successfully

such

suck [sucking sucked]

sucseed   succeed

sucsess   success

suction

sudden   suddenly

sudenley   suddenly

suede *[leather]   swayed *[moved]

sueur   sewer *[drain]

                 sure *[certain]

suffer   sufferer
  [suffering suffered]

sufficient   sufficiently

suffix   suffixes

suffocate   suffocation
  [suffocating suffocated]

suffragette

sufishent   sufficient

sufokate   suffocate

sugar   sugary

suggest [suggesting suggested]

suggestion

suit

suitable   suitably

sulen   sullen

sulk [sulking sulked]   sulkily

sulky   sulkier   sulkiest

sullen   sullenly   sullenness

sultan

sultana

sum *[add]   some *[amount]

sumer   summer

sumersorlt   somersault

sumery   summary
                 *[short]

                 summery
                 *[warm]

summarise [summarised]

summary   summery
      *[outline]   *[warm]

summer   summertime

summit

sumthing   something

sun *[shine]   son *[boy]

sun ~bathe ~burn ~burnt

sun ~flower ~glasses ~lit

sun ~light ~rise ~screen

sun ~set ~shine ~stroke

sun ~tan ~tanned

sundae *[ice cream]

Sunday *[day of week]

sune   soon

sung

sunk   sunken

sunny   sunnier   sunniest

super *[fab]   supper *[meal]

superb   superbly

superhero

superhuman

superior   superiority

supermarket

supersonic

supervise   supervisor

   [supervising supervised]

supervision

suply   supply

suport   support

supose   suppose

supper *[meal]   super *[fab]

suppervise   supervise

supply   supplies

   [supplying supplied]

support   supportive

   [supporting supported]

suppose   supposedly

   [supposing supposed]

supprise   surprise

sure *[certain]   shore *[sea]

surely

surender   surrender

surf *[sea]   serf *[slave]

surface   surfaces

   [surfacing surfaced]

surge [surging surged]

surgeon

surgery   surgeries

surgical   surgically

surly

surmon   sermon

surname

suround   surround

surpent   serpent

surpliing   supplying

surprise   surprisingly

   [surprising surprised]

surrender   surrendered

surround   surroundings

   [surrounding surrounded]

survalence   surveillance

survant   servant

surve   serve

surveillance

survey   surveyor

   [surveying surveyed]

survice   service

surviet   serviette

survival   survivor

survive [surviving survived]

suspect [suspecting suspected]

suspend [suspended]

suspense

suspicion   suspicious

suspiciously

sutch   such

sute   soot *[coal]

                 suit *[clothes]

sutibul   suitable

suvenear   souvenir

swade   suede

swagger [swaggering swaggered]

swallow   swallowed

swam

swamp   swamped   swampy

swan [swanning swanned]

swap [swapping swapped]

swarm *[bees]   swam *[swim]

swat *[hit]   swot *[study]

sway [swaying swayed]

swayd   suede

sweat *[hot]   sweet *[food]

  [sweating sweated]

sweater

sweaty   sweatier   sweatiest

swede *[vegetable]

Swede *[from Sweden]

sweep   sweeper [sweeping swept]

sweet   sweetly   sweetness

sweeten sweetened sweetener

swept

swerve [swerving swerved]

swet   sweat *[hot]

                 sweet *[food]

swetter   sweater

swich   switch

swift   swiftly   swiftness

swim   swimmer

  [swimming swam swum]

swine

swing

swipe [swiping swiped]

switch [switches switching switched]

swivel [swivelling swivelled]

swollen

swollow   swallow

swomp   swamp

swon   swan

swoop [swooping swooped]

swop   swap

sword   ~fish ~sman

swot *[study]   swat *[hit]

swum

swung

swurve   swerve

swyne   swine

swype   swipe

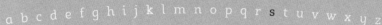

sycul	cycle

Check out cy as well

syclist	cyclist
syclone	cyclone
sygn	sign
sylens	silence
sylent	silent
sylinder	cylinder
syllable	syllabic
syllabus	
symbol *[sign]	cymbal *[music]

symmetrical

sympathetic sympathetically

sympathise

[sympathising sympathised]

sympathy

syncere   sincere

synonym

syrup syrupy

systematic systematically

syte   cite *[quote]

sight *[seeing]

site *[place]

T-shirt

tabby

tabel   table

tabelspoon   tablespoon

table   tablecloth

tablespoon   tablespoonful

tablet

tabloid

tac   take

tack *[nail]   take *[get]

tackle [tackling tackled]

tacks *[pins]   tax *[money]

tacky   tackier   tackiest

tact   tactful   tactfully

tactic   tactical

tactless   tactlessly

tadpole

taek   take

tag [tagging tagged]

t'ai chi

tail *[dog]   tale *[story]

taip   tape

tair   tear

take [taking took taken]

takeaway   takeover

takul   tackle

taks   tax

taksi   taxi

takt   tact

taktik   tactic

tale *[story]   tail *[dog]

talen   talon

talent   talented

talk [talking talked]

talkative

tall   taller   tallest

talon

tame [taming tamed]

tamper [tampering tampered]

tan [tanning tanned]

tang   tangy

tangerine

tangle [tangled]

tanjerine   tangerine

tank

tannoy

tantrum

tap [tapping tapped]

tap-dance   tap-dancing

tape [taping taped]

tapestry   tapestries

tapistry   tapestry

tar [tarred]

tarantula

target [targeting targeted]

tarmac

tarnish [tarnished]

tart   tartness

tartan

task [tasked]

tassel [tasselled]

taste [tasting tasted]

tasteful   tastefully

tasty   tastier   tastiest

tattered   tatters

tattoo   tattoos

tatty   tattier   tattiest

tatu   tattoo

taught *[teach]   taut *[tight]

taunt [taunting taunted]

Taurus

taut *[tight]   taught *[teach]

tawn   torn

tawny

tax [taxes taxing taxed]

taxi   taxis

tea *[drink]   tee *[golf]

teach [teaches teaching taught]

teacher

team *[group]   teem *[swarm]

teanage   teenage

teapot   teaspoon   teatowel

tear *[cry]   tier *[layer]

tear *[rip] [tearing torn]

tearful   tearfully

tease [teasing teased]

Teashert   T-shirt

teaspoon   teaspoonful

techer   teacher

technical   technically

technician

technique

technology

teddy   teddies

tedious

tedy   teddy

tee *[golf]   tea *[drink]

    [tees teeing teed]

teef   teeth

teejuncshun   T-junction

teem *[swarm]   team *[group]

teenage   teenager   teens

teese   tease

Teeshert   T-shirt

teespoon   teaspoon

teeter [teetering teetered]

teeth *[mouth]   teething

teethe *[grow teeth]

tef   teeth

tekneek   technique

tekst   text

telefone   telephone

211

telephone   telephonist

  [telephoning telephoned]

telescope   telescopic

televise [televised]

television

telivise   televise

telivizhun   television

tell [telling told]   teller   telltale

telly

temper   temperamental

temperature

temple

temporary

tempracher   temperature

tempramentl   temperamental

tempt [tempting tempted]

tempul   temple

tempur   temper

ten   tenth

tenant

tend [tended]   tendency

tender tenderly tenderness

tendon

tendur   tender

tenent   tenant

tener   tenner *[£10]

              tenor *[sing]

tenner

tennis

tenor

tenpin bowling

tense [tensed]   tensely

tenshun   tension

tension

tent

tentacle

tenth

tepid

terban   turban

terer   terror

tererise   terrorise

tereybul   terrible

terier   terrier

terific   terrific

teriss   terrace

teritoriel   territorial

terkey   turkey

term [termed]

terminal   terminally

terminate   termination

  [terminating terminated]

termoil   turmoil

Check out
tur as well

terning   turning

212

ternip	turnip
terodactil	pterodactyl
teror	terror
terqwoys	turquoise
terrace	terraced
terracotta	
terrapin	
terrestrial	
terrible	terribly
terrier	
terrific	terrifically
terrify	[terrifies]
	[terrifying terrified]
territorial	
territory	territories
terror	terrorism
terrorise	terrorist
	[terrorising terrorised]
tertle	turtle
test [testing tested]	
testify [testifies testifying testified]	
tether [tethering tethered]	
Tewder	Tudor
tewlip	tulip
tewn	tune
Tewsday	Tuesday
text [texting texted]	
texture	

tey	tea
thach	thatch
than	

Check out F as well

thank [thanking thanked]	
thankful	thankfully
thankless	thanklessly
thank you	
that	
thatch [thatched]	
thaw [thawing thawed]	
thay	they
the	
theat	that
theatre	theatrical
theef	thief
thees	these
theft	
their *[own]	there *[place]
theirs *[owns]	there's *[there is]
theis	these
them	themselves
theme [themed]	
then	
theory	theories
ther	there

213

therapy   therapist

there *[place]   their *[own]

                     they're *[they

                              are]

therefore

there's *[there is] theirs *[owns]

therfour   therefore

thermometer

thers   there's *[there is]

                    theirs *[owns]

Thersday   Thursday

thes   these

these

they

they'd [they had, would]

they'll [they will, shall]

they're *[they   there *[place]

        are]   their *[own]

they've [they have]

thick   thicker   thickest

thicken [thickening thickened]

thicket

thickly   thickness

thief   thieves

thier   there *[place]

                    their *[own]

thigh

thik   thick

thimble   thimbleful

thin   thinner   thinnest

thing

think   thinker [thinking thought]

thinly   thinness

thir   their

third   thirdly

thirst   thirsty   thirstier

thirteen   thirteenth

thirty   thirtieth

this

thistle

thogh   though

thore   thaw

thorn   thorny   thornier

thorough   thoroughly

thoroughbred

thoroughness

thort   thought

thorteen   fourteen

thortless   thoughtless

those

though

thought   thought-provoking

thoughtful   thoughtfully

thoughtfulness

thoughtless   thoughtlessly

thoughtlessness

thousand   thousandth

thow   though

thowsand   thousand

thrash [thrashing thrashed]

thread   threadbare
  [threading threaded]

threat

threaten [threatening threatened]

thred   thread

three   three-dimensional

thret   threat

thretton   threaten

threw *[ball]   through *[via]

thrill [thrilling thrilled]

thrive [thriving thrived throve]

throat   throaty

throb [throbbing throbbed]

throne *[king]   thrown *[ball]

throng [thronging thronged]

throo   through

throttle [throttled]

through *[via]   threw *[ball]

throughout

throw *[ball]   through *[via]
  [throwing threw thrown]

thrown *[ball]   throne *[king]

thrush   thrushes

thrust [thrusting thrust]

thud [thudding thudded]

thum   thumb

thumb [thumbing thumbed]

thump [thumping thumped]

thunder   thundery
  [thundering thundered]

thurmometur   thermometer

Thursday

thus

thwart [thwarted]

thwort   thwart

thyme *[herb]   time *[clock]

tiara

tic *[twitch]   tick *[clock,
  [ticking ticked]   mark]

ticket

tickle   ticklish [tickling tickled]

tidal

tiddlywinks

tide *[sea]   tied *[up]

tidy   tidier   tidiest

tie *[up]   Thai *[Thailand]

tie [ties tying tied]

tie chee   t'ai chi

tied *[up]   tide *[sea]

tier *[layer]   tear *[cry]

                      tire *[sleep]

                      tyre *[wheel]

215

tifoon   typhoon
tifoyd   typhoid
tiger   tigress
tight   tighter   tightly
tighten [tightening tightened]
tik   tick
tikul   tickle
tile
till *[until, shop]
tilt [tilting tilted]
timber
time *[clock]   thyme *[herb]
  [timing timed]
time   ~less ~table
timid   timidity   timidly
tin   tinned
tinge [tinged]
tingle [tingling tingled]
tinker [tinkering tinkered]
tinkle [tinkling tinkled]
tinsel   tinselly
tint [tinting tinted]
tiny   tinier   tiniest
tip *[advice]   type *[sort]
tiperiter   typewriter
tipes   types
tipical   typical
tiptoe [tiptoeing tiptoed]

tirannosaurus   tyrannosaurus
tirant   tyrant
tire *[sleep]   tyre *[wheel]
tire [tiring tired]
tireless   tirelessly
tirn   turn
tirteen   thirteen
tishue   tissue
tissue
tit *[bird]   tight *[firm]
titbit
tite   tight
title [titled]
titter [tittering tittered]
tiyed   tired
to *[do]   too *[also]
                  two *[number]
toad *[frog]   towed *[pulled]
toadstool
toan   tone
toast [toasted]
tobacco   tobacconist
toboggan
  [tobogganing tobogganed]
today
toddle [toddling toddled]   toddler
tode   toad *[frog]
                  towed *[pulled]

todel   toddle

toe *[foot]   tow *[pull]

toffee   toffees

toga

together   togetherness

toil [toiling toiled]

toilet   toiletries

token

toksic   toxic

told

toled   told

tolerable   tolerably

tolerait   tolerate

tolerance   tolerant

tolerate [tolerating tolerated]

toll [tolling tolled]

tolrabul   tolerable

tom   ~boy ~cat

tomato   tomatoes

tomb   tombstone

tombola

tomeake   tummy ache

tommow   tomorrow

tomorrow

ton *[imperial]   tonne *[metric]

tone   toneless

tongs

tongue

tonic

tonight

tonne *[metric]   ton *[imperial]

tonsil   tonsilitis

too *[also]   to *[do]

two *[2]

tooc   took

toocan   toucan

toogever   together

took

tool   toolkit

toom   tomb

toopay   toupée

toot [tooting tooted]

tooth   ~ache ~brush

tooth   ~less ~paste ~pick

toothy

tootifrooti   tutti-frutti

top [topping topped]

topic   topical

topple [toppled]

topsy-turvy

torch   torchlight

torcher   torture

torist   tourist

tork   talk

torment   tormentor

[tormenting tormented]

torn

tornado   tornadoes

tornament   tournament

torney   tawny

tornt   taunt

torpedo   torpedoes

[torpedoing torpedoed]

torrent   torrential

Torrus   Taurus

tortoise   tortoiseshell

tortoys   tortoise

torture   torturer

[torturing tortured]

tortuss   tortoise

Tory   Tories

toss [tossing tossed]

tost   toast

total   totally

totem pole

totter [tottering tottered]

toucan

touch [touches touching touched]

touchy   touchier   touchiest

tough   tougher   toughest

toughen [toughened]

toughness

toupée

tour *[journey]   tore *[rip]

tourist   touristy   tourism

tournament

Tousday   Tuesday

tow *[pull]   toe *[foot]

[towing towed]

toward   towards

towed *[pulled]   toad *[frog]

towel   towelling

tower [towering towered]

towle   towel

town

toxic   toxin

toy

toylet   toilet

trabl   trouble

trace   traceable   tracing

track [tracking tracked]

tractor

trade [trading traded]

tradesman

tradishun   tradition

tradition   traditional

traffic

tragedy   tragedies

tragic   tragically

traid   trade

trail [trailing trailed]

train   trainer [training trained]

trais	trace
traitor	
trajedy	tragedy
trajic	tragic
trak	track
trale	trail
tram	
tramp [tramped]	
trample [trampled]	
trampoline trampolining	
trance	
trane	train
tranquil tranquility	
tranquilliser [tranquillised]	
transatlantic	
transe	trance
transfer [transferring transferred]	
transform transformation	
[transforming transformed]	
transishun	transition
transition	
translate translation	
[translating translated]	
transmishun	transmission
transmission	
transmit [transmitted]	
transparent transparency	
transplant [transplanted]	

transport [transported]	
trap [trapping trapped]	
trapeze	
trapezium trapezoid	
trash trashed trashy	
trauma traumatic	
travel traveller	
[travelling travelled]	
travler	traveller
trawler	
tray	
traytor	traitor
treacherous treacherously	
treachery	
treacle	
tread [treading trod trodden]	
treason treasonable	
treasure treasurer	
[treasuring treasured]	
treasury	
treat [treating treated]	
treatment	
treaty treaties	
treble	
trecherus	treacherous
trechery	treachery
tred	tread
tree trees	

219

treeo   trio

treet   treat

treety   treaty

trek [trekking trekked]

tremble [trembling trembled]

tremendous   tremendously

tremor

trench   trenches

trend   trendy   trendier

treshere   treasure

trespass   trespasses

trew   true

trewansy   truancy

trewly   truly

trewthful   truthful

trial

triangle   triangular

triathlon

tribal   tribe   tribes

tributary   tributaries

tribute

triceps

trick [tricked]   trickery

trickle [trickling trickled]

tricky   trickier   trickiest

tricycle

tried

trifle

triggard   triggered

trigger [triggered]

triing   trying

trik   trick

trikel   trickle

trile   trial

trilogy

trim [trimming trimmed]

trio

trip [tripping tripped]

tripet   tripped

triple   triplets

triseps   triceps

triumph   triumphant

trivial

troble   trouble

trod   trodden

trofee   trophy

troff   trough

troll

trolley   trollies

trombone   trombonist

troop [trooping trooped]

trophy   trophies

tropic   tropical

trorma   trauma

trot [trotting trotted]

trouble [troubling troubled]

troublemaker   troublesome

trough

trousers

trout

trowel

trowser   trouser

truancy   truant

trubbel   trouble

truce

truck   trucker   trucking

trudge [trudging trudged]

true

truj   trudge

truly

trumpet [trumpeted]

truncheon

trundle [trundling trundled]

trunk

trupeez   trapeze

trust [trusting trusted]

trustworthy   trusty

truth   truthful   truthfully

truthfulness

try [tries trying tried]

trycycle   tricycle

tryed   tried

tryumf   triumph

tsar   tsarina

T-shirt

tsunami   tsunamis

tub   tubby   tubbier

tube   tubular

tuberculosis

tuch   touch

tuck [tucking tucked]

tuct   tucked

Tudor

Tuesday

tuffen   toughen

tuft   tufted   tufty

tug [tugging tugged]

tuition

tuk   took *[take]

          tuck *[in]

tule   tool

tulip

tumble [tumbling tumbled]

tume   tomb

tummy   tummyache

tumour

tumy   tummy

tuna

tune [tuning tuned]

tuneful   tunefully

tung   tongue

tunic

tunnel   tunneller

[tunnelling tunnelled]

tupay   toupée

turban

turbulence   turbulent

turf [turfed]

turkey *[bird]

Turkey *[country]   Turkish

turm   term

Check out
ter as well

turmoil

turn [turning turned]

turnip

turquoise

turrestrial   terrestrial

turret

turtle   turtledove

Tusday   Tuesday

tusk

tussle [tussling tussled]

tuth   tooth

tutor   tutorial

tutti-frutti

tuword   toward

twang [twanging twanged]

tweak [tweaking tweaked]

tweed   tweedy

tweek   tweak

tweet [tweeting]

tweezers

twelth   twelfth

twelve   twelfth

twente   twenty

twentieth

twenty   twenty-first

twerl   twirl

twevl   twelve

twice

twiddle [twiddling twiddled]

twig [twigged]

twilight

twin *[two]   [twinned]

twine *[string]   [twined]

twinge [twinged]

twinkle [twinkling twinkled]

twirl [twirling twirled]

twise   twice

twist [twisting twisted]

twisty   twistier   twistiest

twit

twitch   twitches   twitchy

[twitching twitched]

twitter   twittery

[twittering twittered]

two *[2]

twurl

twylight

ty

tyara

tyde

tying

tyme

type

to *[in order to]

too *[also, very]

twirl

twilight

tie

tiara

tide *[sea]

tied *[up]

time *[clock]

thyme *[herb]

typewriter   typist

  [typing typed]

typhoon

typhoid

typical   typically

tyrannise   [tyrannised]

tyrannosaurus rex

tyrant

tyre *[wheel]   tire *[sleep]

tytan   tighten

Check out
ti as well

ubout	about
udder	
uftaer	after
ugane	again
ugh	
ugly uglier ugliest	
ule	Yule
uliteration	alliteration
ulser	ulcer
ultraviolet	
umbrella	
umpire *[game]	empire *[lands]
[umpired]	
unable	enable
*[not able]	*[to make able]
unacceptable	
unaccompanied	
unaccustomed	
unaided	
unappetising	
unarmed	
unaversil	universal
unavoidable	
unaware	
unbearable unbearably	
unbelievable unbelievably	
unblock [unblocking unblocked]	
uncertain uncertainly	

uncertainty
unchanged
uncivilised
uncle
unconscious   unconsciously
unconsciousness
uncontrollable
uncontrollably
unconvincing
uncover [uncovering uncovered]
undecided
undeniable   undeniably
under   ~cover ~graduate
under   ~ground ~growth ~hand
under   ~neath ~study ~wear
underestimate
underline [underlined]
undermine [undermined]
understand
   [understanding understood]
understandable
understandably
undertake   undertaker
   [undertaking undertook undertaken]
undesirable
undignified
undiniabel   undeniable
undo [undoing undid undone]

undoubted   undoubtedly

undrinkable

unearth   unearthly
  [unearthing unearthed]

uneasy   uneasier

uneatable   uneaten

unecessary   unnecessary

uneducated

uneek   unique

unekspected   unexpected

unemotional

unemployable

unemployed   unemployment

unenthusiastic

unequal   unequally

unequalled

unerth   unearth

uneven   unevenly

unexciting

unexpected   unexpectedly

unfair   unfairly   unfairness

unfaithful

unfamiliar

unfashionable   unfashionably

unfernished   unfurnished

unfinished

unflattering

unforeseeable

unforgettable

unforgivable

unfortunate   unfortunately

unfrendly   unfriendly

unfriendly

unfurnished

ungarded   unguarded

ungrateful   ungratefully

unhappiness   unhappily

unhappy unhappier unhappiest

unhealthy   unhealthier

unheard of

unien   union

unicorn

uniform

unimaginable

unimportant

uninhabited

unintentional

unintentionally

unintresting   uninteresting

uninterested   uninteresting

union *[join]   onion *[veg]

Union Jack

unique   uniquely   uniqueness

unisex

unit

unite [uniting united]

225

unity

universal   universally

universe

university   universities

unjust   unjustly

unkind   unkinder   unkindest

unkindly   unkindness

unkle   uncle

unknown   unknowingly

unleaded

unless

unlike   unlikely

unlovable   unloved

unlucky   unluckiest

unmanned

unmarked

unmistakable   unmistakably

unmoved

unnatural   unnaturally

unnecessary

unnown   unknown

unpaid

unpleasant   unpleasantly

unpleasantness

unplug [unplugged]

unpopular   unpopularity

unprepared

unpripared   unprepared

unprotected

unraliabul   unreliable

unrap   unwrap

unravel [unravelling unravelled]

unreal   unrealistic

unreasonable   unreasonably

unreliable

unritten   unwritten

unruly   unrulier   unruliest

unscramble [unscrambled]

unscrew [unscrewing unscrewed]

unsed   unsaid

unseen

unselfish   unselfishly

unselfishness

unsertain   uncertain

unshakeable

unsientific   unscientific

unsightly

unsivilised   uncivilised

unskilled

unskrew   unscrew

unsociable

unsolved

unsoshabul   unsociable

unspeakable

unspoken

unsporting

unsteady   unsteadily
unsuccessful
unsuccessfully
unsuitable   unsuited
untidy   untidier   untidiest
untie [untying untied]
until
untold
untrustworthy
untruthful
unusable
unusual   unusually
unuther   another
unwelcome   unwelcoming
unwrap [unwrapping unwrapped]
unwritten
unyun   onion *[veg]
               union *[flag]
unyvers   universe
unzip [unzipping unzipped]
up   ~beat ~right
upbringing
upgrade [upgraded]
upheaval
upheval   upheaval
uplift [uplifting uplifted]
upon
upper

uprising
uprite   upright
uproar
upset [upsetting]
upshot
upside-down
upstairs
uptight
uptite   uptight
upward   upwards
upwood   upward
uranium
Uranus
urban
urchin
Urdu
ure   your
urge [urging urged]
urgent   urgently   urgency
urine
urly   early

Check out
ear as well

urn *[vase]   earn *[money]
urnest   earnest
Uropean   European
urth   earth

227

us

use [using used]   user

usable   usage

useful   usefully   usefulness

useless   uselessly

uselessness

userp   usurp

usher [ushering ushered]

uskt   asked

usual   usually

usurp [usurped]   usurper

utensil

uther   other

utmost

utter [uttering uttered]

utterly

uver   other

uvm   oven

uway   away

uze   use

uzual   usual

V-neck   V-necked

vacancy   vacancies

vacant   vacantly

vaccinate   vaccination
  [vaccinating vaccinated]

vacuum [vacuuming vacuumed]

vael   vale *[valley]

              veil *[cloth]

vage   vague

vague   vaguely   vagueness

vain *[proud]   vein *[blood]

              vane *[weather]

vaiporise   vaporise

vakansy   vacancy

vakant   vacant

vaksinate   vaccinate

vaksine   vaccine

vakuum   vacuum

valay   valley

valentine

valew   value

valley   valleys

valuable

value   values

valuntine   valentine

valve

valyu   value

vampire

van

vandal   vandalism

vandalise [vandalised]

vane *[weather]   vain *[proud]

              vein *[blood]

vanilla

vanish [vanishing vanished]

vanity

vaper   vapour

vaporise [vaporised]

vapour

variable

varied

variety   varieties

various   variously

varnish [varnishing varnished]

varse   vase

vary *[change]   very *[much]
  [varying varied]

vase

vast   vastly   vastness

Vatican

vault

vayn   vain *[proud]

              vane *[weather]

              vein *[blood]

veal

vector

vegetable

vegetarian   veggie

vegetation

vegtabul   vegetable

vehicle

veikel   vehicle

veil *[cloth]   vale *[valley]

vein *[blood]   vain *[proud]

                    vane *[weather]

veiw   view

vejetabul   vegetable

vejetarian   vegetarian

velocity

velvet   velvety

vencher   venture

vendetta

vending machine

vendor

venew   venue

Venn diagram

venom   venomous

vent [venting vented]

ventilate [ventilating ventilated]

ventilation   ventilator

ventriloquist

venture [venturing ventured]

venue

venum   venom

Venus

veray   very

verb   verbal   verbally

verbalise

vercabulary   vocabulary

verdict

verge

veriety   variety

verius   various

vermin

verruca   verrucas

verse

verses *[poem]   versus *[against]

version

versus *[against]   verses *[poem]

vertebra   vertebrae

vertebrate

vertex   vertices

vertical   vertically

vertigo

vertu   virtue

vertual   virtual

vertuos   virtuous

very *[much]   vary *[change]

vessel

vest

vet   veterinary

veteran

veto   vetoes [vetoed]

via

vialens   violence

vibe   vibration

vibrate [vibrating vibrated]

vicar   vicarage

vice   vice-president

vice versa

vicious   viciously

victim

victimise [victimising victimised]

victor

Victorian

victorious   victoriously

victory   victories

video   videos

vidio   video

vielence   violence

view [viewing viewed]

vigger   vigour

vigilance

vigilant   vigilantly

vigorous   vigorously

vigour

vikar   vicar

Viking

viksen   vixen

viktim   victim

viktimise   victimise

vile

vilense   violence

vilige   village

villa

village   villager

villain   villainous   villainy

vinager   vinegar

vinaigrette

vine   vineyard

vinegar   vinegary

vintage

violence   violent   violently

violet

violin   violinist

viper

virb   verb

Check out
ver as well

virge   verge

virgin

Virgo

virjin   virgin

virse   verse

virtual   virtually

virtue   virtuous

virus   viruses

visa

visable   visible

vishus   vicious

visible visibility visibly

vision

visit [visiting visited]

visitor

visor

visual visually

visualise visualisation
   [visualising visualised]

vital vitality vitally

vitamin

vivid vividly vividness

vixen

vniler   vanilla

voat   vote

vocabulary

vocal vocalist vocally

vocation vocational

voice [voicing voiced]

void

vokabulary   vocabulary

volcano volcanoes volcanic

vole

volkano   volcano

volley volleyball

volnteerd   volunteered

volt voltage

volume

voluntary voluntarily

volunteer [volunteered]

vomit [vomiting vomited]

vorlt   vault

vote [voting voted]

vouch vouched voucher

vow [vowing vowed]

vowel

voyage voyager

voys   voice

vue   view

vulcher   vulture

vulgar

vulnerable

vulture

vunrabel   vulnerable

vurb   verb

Check out **ver** as well

vurge   verge

vurse   verse

vurtuel   virtual

vya   via

wack	whack	waken [wakening wakened]	
wacks	wax	waks	wax
wad *[pad]	wade *[water]	Wales *[place]	whales *[sea]
waddle [waddling waddled]		walk [walking walked]	
wade *[water]	weighed *[load]	walk	~about ~over ~way
[wading waded]		walker	
wafer	wafer-thin	walkie-talkie	
waffle		wall [walled]	
wag [wagging wagged]		wallaby	wallabies
wage [waging waged]		wallet	
wager		wallop [walloping walloped]	
waggle [waggling waggled]		wallow [wallowing wallowed]	
wagon		walnut	
waht	what	walrus	walruses
waid	wade *[water]	waltz	waltzes
	weighed *[load]	wand	
waifer	wafer	wander *[roam]	wonder *[think]
wail *[cry]	whale *[sea]	[wandering wandered]	
[wailing wailed]		want [wanting wanted]	
waist *[body]	waste *[misuse]	war *[battle]	wore *[dress]
waist	~band ~coat ~line	war	~fare ~like ~ship ~time
wait *[delay]	weight *[load]	ward [warding warded]	
[waiting waited]		warden	
waiter	waitress	wardrobe	
waiting room		warehouse	[warehousing]
waj	wage	wares *[goods]	wears *[coat]
wake [waking woke woken]		warm [warming warmed]	
wakeful		warm-hearted	

warmth   warmly

warn *[alert]   worn *[old]
  [warning warned]

warren

warrior

wart   warthog

wary   warier   wariest

was

wash [washing washed]

wash   ~basin ~out ~room

washer   washing

wasn't [was not]

wasp   waspish

wastage

waste *[misuse]   waist *[body]

wasteful   wastefully

wasteland

watch [watches watching watched]

watch   ~dog ~man

watchful   watchfully

water [watering watered]

water   ~colour ~cress ~fall

water   ~front ~logged

water   ~melon ~side ~tight

waterproof [waterproofed]

water-ski   water-skiing

watery

watt *[power]   what *[?]

watter   water

wave [waving waved]

wave   ~band ~length

wavy   wavier   waviest

wax [waxes waxing waxed]

waxwork

way *[track]   weigh *[load]

waykn   waken

wayt   wait *[delay]

            weight *[load]

we *[us]   wee *[tiny]

weak *[feeble]   week *[7 days]

weaken

  [weakening weakened]

weaker   weakest

weakly *[feebly]   weekly
                *[every week]

weakness

weal *[mark]   wheel *[car]

            we'll
                *[we will, shall]

wealth

wealthy wealthier wealthiest

weapon

wear *[dress]   were *[be]

            where *[place]

            weir *[dam]

wearily   weariness

234

weard — weird

wears *[coat]   wares *[goods]

weary wearier weariest

weasel

weather *[sun, rain] whether *[if]
 [weathering weathered]

weather-beaten

weave *[cloth]   we've *[we have]
 [weaving wove woven]

webbed

we'd *[we had,   weed *[plant]
  would]

wed *[married]

wedding

Wedensday   Wednesday

wedge [wedging wedged]

Wednesday

weed *[plant]   we'd *[we had,
 [weeding weeded]   would]

weedy weedier weediest

week *[7 days]   weak *[feeble]

weekend

weekly *[every week]
 weakly *[feebly]

weel   weal *[mark]
    wheel *[car]

weep [weeping wept]

weesal   weasel

weet   wheat

weeze   wheeze

weigh *[load]   way *[track]

weight *[load]   wait *[delay]

weight weightless

weightlessness

weight ~lifter ~lifting

weight training

weild   wield

weir *[dam]   wear *[dress]

weird weirder weirdest

weirdly weirdness

wej   wedge

welcome [welcoming welcomed]

weld [welding welded]

welfare

well better best

well-behaved

well-known

well-mannered

wellington boot

welth   wealth

wen   when

Wensday   Wednesday

went

wept

werd   weird *[strange]
    word *[speech]

were *[be]   whirr *[sound]

we're *[we are]   weir *[dam]

weren't [were not]

werewolf   werewolves

werk   work

werl   whirl

werld   world

werr   were *[be]

                    whirr *[sound]

west ~bound ~erly ~ern

westwards

wet [wetting wetted]

wet   wetness

wether   weather *[sun]

                    whether *[if]

we've *[we have] weave *[cloth]

whack [whacking whacked]

whacks *[hits]   wax *[candle]

whale *[sea]   wail *[cry]

whaling

what *[?]   watt *[power]

what   whatever

whatsoever

wheat

wheel *[car]   weal *[mark]

  [wheeling wheeled]

wheel ~barrow ~chair

wheeze   wheezy

  [wheezing wheezed]

when   whenever

whent   went

wher   where

where *[place]   wear *[dress]

                    were *[be]

whereabouts

whereas

whereupon

wherever

whether *[if]   weather

                          *[sun]

whey *[milk]   way *[track]

which *[?]   witch *[hag]

whichever

whiff

while   whilst

whim

whimper [whimpering whimpered]

whine *[moan]   wine *[drink]

whined *[moaned]   wind *[turn]

whip *[beat] [whipping whipped]

whippet

whirl [whirling whirled]

whirl ~pool ~wind

whirr *[sound]   were *[be]

  [whirring whirred]

whisk [whisking whisked]

whisker   whiskery

whisper [whispering whispered]

whistle [whistling whistled]

white   whiter   whitest

whitish   whiteness

whiz [whizzes whizzing whizzed]

who *[?]   hew *[cut]

who'd *[who had, would]

whoever

whole *[full]   hole *[gap]

whole   ~food ~hearted ~meal

who'll *[who will]

wholly *[fully]   holy *[God]

                    holey *[holes]

whom   whomever

whood   would

whooping cough

whopper   whopping

who're *[who are]

who's *[who is, has]

whose *[belongs]

who've *[who have]

why

wi   why

wich   which *[?]

                    witch *[hag]

wicked   wickeder   wickedest

wickedly   wickedness

wicket   ~keeper

wide   wider   widest

widely

widen [widening widened]

widespread

widow   widower

width

wield [wielding wielded]

wier   weir *[dam]

                    we're *[we are]

wierd   weird

wiery   weary

wife   wives

wig

wiggle [wiggling wiggled]

wiggly

wigwam

wikid   wicked

wild   wilder   wildest

wilderness   wildernesses

wildly   wildness

wilful   wilfully   wilfulness

will

willing   willingly   willingness

willow   willowy

wilt [wilting wilted]

wily   wilier   wiliest

wim   whim

wimen   women

wimper   whimper

win [winning won]

wince [wincing winced]

winch [winches]

   [winching winched]

wind *[turn]   whined

   [winding wound]   *[moaned]

wind *[air]

wind   ~fall ~mill ~pipe

wind   ~screen ~surfer

window   ~pane

windy   windier   windiest

wine *[drink]   whine *[moan]

wing [winged]

wing · wingspan

wink [winking winked]

winner   winnings

winter   ~time

wintry

wipe [wiping wiped]

wiper

wire [wiring wired]

wire   wireless

wirlwind   whirlwind

wisdom

wise   wiser   wisest

wisell   whistle

wisely

wish [wishing wished]

wishful   wishfully

wisk   whisk

          whisker

wisp   wispy

wisper   whisper

wistful   wistfully

wit

witch *[hag]   which *[?]

witchcraft   witches

with   within

wither [withering withered]

without

witness [witnessed]

witnesses

witty   wittier   wittiest

wizard   wizardry

wnet   went

wobble [wobbling wobbled]

wobbly

woch   watch

Check out
wa as well

wod   wad *[pad]

          word *[speech]

238

woffel	waffle
woft	waft
woke woken	
wolf wolves	
wollaby	wallaby
wollet	wallet
wollop	wallop
wollow	wallow
woltz	waltz
woman women	
womb	
won *[victory]	one *[number]
wond	wand
wonder *[think]	wander *[roam]
[wondering wondered]	
wonderful wonderfully	
wons	once
wont	want
won't *[will not]	
wood *[trees]	would *[would go]
wooded	
wooden	
woodlouse	
wood ~land ~pecker ~wind	
wood ~work ~worm	
wool woollen woolly	
woom	womb
wopper	whopper

wor	war *[battle]
	wore *[clothes]
word [wording worded]	
word-processor	
wordy wordier wordiest	
wore *[clothes] war *[hit]	
work [working worked]	
workable	
work ~load ~man ~shop	
workitorkie	walkie-talkie
worl	wall
worlrus	walrus
world worldwide	
World War I	
World War II	
worm [worming wormed]	
worn *[used]	warn *[alert]
worpt	warped
worrant	warrant
worrior	warrior
worry [worries worrying worried]	
wors	wars
worse worst	
worsen [worsening worsened]	
worship	
[worshipping worshipped]	
worst	
wort	wart

239

worter   water

worth   worthless   worthwhile

worthy   worthier   worthiest

wos   was

wosh   wash

wosnt   wasn't

wosp   wasp

wot   watt *[power]

     what *[?]

wotch   watch

would *[would go] wood *[trees]

wouldn't *[would not]

wound *[hurt]

   [wounding wounded]

wove   woven

wow

wownd   wound *[clock]

woz   was

wrap *[pack]   rap *[pop, knock]

   [wrapping wrapped]

wreath

wreck [wrecking wrecked]

wreckage

wren

wrench [wrenches]

   [wrenching wrenched]

wrestle   wrestler

   [wrestling wrestled]

wretch *[rogue]   retch *[sick]

wretched   wretches

wriggle [wriggling wriggled]

wriggly

wrighting   writing

> Check out R as well

wring *[wet]   ring *[circle, bell]

  [wringing wrung]

wrinkle   wrinkled   wrinkly

wrist   wristwatch

write *[pen]   right *[exact]

     rite *[act]

writer [writing wrote written]

writhe [writhing writhed]

wrong   wrongfully   wrongly

wronged

wrote *[text]   rote *[learn]

wrung   rung

     *[squeezed]   *[ladder, bell]

wry *[humour]   rye *[grain]

wryly

wu   woo

wud   wood *[trees]

     would *[would go]

wuff   woof

wulf   wolf

wull	**wool**	wurld	**world**
wully	**woolly**	wurldwide	**worldwide**
wuman	**woman**	wurr	**were** *[we were
wume	**womb**		late]
wunder	**wonder** *[think]		**whirr** *[sound]
wurd	**word**	wuz	**was**
wuren't	**weren't** [were	wyde	**wide**
	not]	wyfe	**wife**
wurk	**work**	wyle	**while** *[when]
wurl	**whirl**		**wile** *[trick]

X-ray   X-rays

  [x-raying x-rayed]

xma   eczema

Xmas

xylophone

Check out
ex as well

yacht   yachting

yachtsman   yachtswoman

yak

yam

yank [yanking yanked]

yap [yapping yapped]

yard

yashmak

yaun   yawn

yawn [yawning yawned]

yeah

year   yearly

yeast

yeer   year

yeest   yeast

yeh   yeah

yeild   yield

yeld   yelled

yell [yelling yelled]

yellow   yellower   yellowest

yellowish

yelo   yellow

yelp [yelping yelped]

yen

yer   year

yere   year

yes

yesterday

yet

yeti

yew *[tree]   ewe *[sheep]

                       you *[person]

yews *[trees]   use *[apply]

yield [yielding yielded]

yippee

yoak   yoke *[round
                              neck]

                       yolk *[egg]

yodel [yodelling yodelled]

yoga

yogert   yoghurt

yoghurt

yolk *[egg]   yoke *[neck]

yoow   you

yorn   yawn

yors   yours

yorself   yourself

yot   yacht

you *[person]   yew *[tree]

                       ewe *[sheep]

you'd *[you had, would]

youf   youth

you'll *[you will]   Yule *[Xmas]

young   youngster

youniform   uniform

your *[owns]   you're *[you are]

yours faithfully

yours sincerely

yourself   yourselves

yous   use

you'sd   used

youth   youthful

youth hostel

you've *[you have]

yo-yo

yu   yew *[tree]

                    you *[person]

yud   you'd *[you had,
                             would]

Yule *[Xmas]   you'll *[you will]

yummy   yum-yum

yung   young

yunger   younger

yuse   use

yuth   youth

zap [zapping zapped]

zapper

zeal zealous

zebra zebra-crossing

zeel   zeal

zero zeros

zest

zigzag
  [zigzagging zigzagged]

zilophone   xylophone

Zimmer™-frame

zinc

zip [zipping zipped]

ziro   zero

zoan   zone

zodiac

zombie

zone [zoning zoned]

zonked

zoo zoo-keeper

Zoolu   Zulu

zoom [zooming zoomed]

zoom lens

zu   zoo

Zulu

zylofone   xylophone